New Haven

Adam Kirstein, M.D.

DEDICATION

To my lovely wife Alena. Mwah.
To my family, my friends, my cats.
To you, the reader: Without literature, there is no history. Without history,
there is no future.

CONTENTS

ACKNOWLEDGMENTS

Richell Designs- Book Cover Art

Mar Fenech- Developmental Editing

Eden Gabay- Audible Production

Alena Kirstein, Jacob Kirstein, Joshua Kirstein, Bonnie Lambert, Steven Kirstein, Chuck Lambert, Rachelle Perl- Advice

Mrs. Stream- High School English Teacher- Encouragement

Hashem

CHAPTER 0

Helicopter blades furiously chop through the air sending shockwaves to the ground that is quickly approaching just 10 feet below. Strong gusts of wind kick up dust from the ground, bouncing debris off the tiny little house that sits alone on the hill. The house is made of rotten tanned wood. Inhabited by termites and carpenter bees for decades. It appears empty.

"Fuck me. They're here," says Howard. "Kids. Get to the hideaway. You two," he says, pointing at his newest rescues. "With me."

Howard guides Stephy and Greg Jalkower to a pantry in the kitchen.

"Get in here and don't make a sound," he says, cramming them into the closet.

Howard takes a beat to make eye contact with the poor young couple he is trying to salvage from a cruel, cruel world. He stares into their eyes.

"Thank you," Stephy whispers as the door is quickly shut in her face.

Howard runs across the living room from the kitchen and places the rug back on top of the trap door to the hideaway. Just as the last corner of the rug touches the ground, trampling footsteps bellow outside.

Howard rushes over to the kitchen drawer and produces a small revolver. His hands shake violently as he spins the cartridge revealing only 3 bullets. He opens the refrigerator door and steps inside.

The shelving has been removed and plumbing hasn't worked for months. It's a perfect space to fit a body if you don't mind the smell of rotten eggs and decaying rationed lunch meat. Howard plugs his nose.

The front door to the wooden house opens slowly. The old door squeals as it sways. Howard holds his breath.

The floor creaks as military boots give their weight. The sounds get louder.

"Howard!" yells a voice. "Howard we just want to talk."

Silence.

"Howard, it's been some time, hasn't it?" Asks the voice, as more footsteps trail behind it.

The creeping sounds of boots on hardened flooring get louder. Closer to the fridge. Then stop.

"Check the rooms," the voice instructs.

"You, over there. Look around. Find me this son of a bitch."

Howard closes his eyes. His breath is short and quiet. He is doing his best to maintain his composure. He has been through this before.

The footsteps trudge away from the fridge and deeper into the kitchen.

He's going for the closet.

He hears boots trailing away from the voice as it gives instructions on where to search.

There's probably 4 or 5 of them by the sounds of it. They're separating.

Howard opens the fridge door silently. The hinges are perfectly greased. He sees the back of a tall and husky man in Leadership uniform creeping slowly toward the pantry. He recognizes the man immediately.

Howard looks around quickly. It's clear. Just the sounds of rummaging from the bedrooms.

The man is directly in front of the pantry now. He reaches out his hand to open the door when the sound of a cocked hammer stops him in his place.

"Fuck off Bryan."

BOOM

Howard takes one shot, folding Bryan to the ground as a single bullet enters his brain. He takes off with haste toward the open door to the outside. Howard unlatches the helicopter door and enters a code into the reader. The blades begin to swing.

He cocks the hammer back to load the next round as two members of leadership appear at the doorway screaming.

"Traitor!" They howl at him as they aim their rifles.

Howard shoots at the door as the aircraft lifts into the air. Bullets are returned, narrowly missing him but striking one of the landing sticks at the bottom of the helicopter. Howard escapes and with one bullet to spare.

Under the hideaway, Francie and David are crammed into a tight space.

"Can you breathe?" asks Francie.

"Yeah. I think so."

"Ok, it will be over soon. I think dad got away again."

"You don't always have to take care of me you know," whispers David.

"I'm your big sister. That's my job."

David scrunches his face.

"You know what happens if we get caught don't you."

"Yes!" says David. Clearly annoyed.

"Ok. What?"

"They'll make us get weird jobs and take all our money and control everything. I'm not an idiot."

"Your right," says Francie. But you're only twelve years old. You still need me and dad.

"I know," says David crossing his arms. "Why do they do this to us anyway? Why can't we just choose how we live our lives?"

Francie sighs. "Dad says it's just human behavior. He says when humans get too much power, they abuse it.

"Abuse it?" asks David.

"Yeah. Sometimes the monster just gets so big, you can't beat it. They make it seem like you're just living in a normal world. Everything is good. Taken care of. When really, they know everything you're doing. They control everything you see. Everything you hear. Everything you do. There's no more thoughts, opinions, or heroes. Just Leadership, regular people, and traitors."

"And were the traitors?" David asks.

.

1 IN THE BEGINNING

2096

~~Manhattan~~ New Haven

To be great is to be good. To live is to serve. To obey is to be free, reads a large poster inside of The Workplace. James studies the letters as if he is trying to understand the true meaning of the message. It has been some time since he thought about something other than work. He remembers things being different. Before New Haven, before the Green Grass, before The Regiment had taken power fifteen years ago.

Before things were good. And they *are* good.

One no longer has to worry about things that used to present challenges. Every bill accounted for and paid. Every check processed in a central bank account and loaded on a person card or PC. No jail, no police, no laws. Only The Way as it's called.

The Way is more than a saying. A strict law of habitation, an iron fist, of sorts. Everyone lives The Way without exception.

Before the Regiment came to power, society thirsted for freedom and for structure. The people demanded a new way. Something to help them cope with their primal instincts being pushed over for political correctness and their voices left unheard. Now there's only one voice.

A loud, shrill sound breaks through James' thoughts. "James, get in here this instant."

Tom is the manager of this 3rd floor subsection of the workplace. Despite his towering height, he could hardly fill out his clothing as he seems to get skinnier by the hour. He has a short stubby nose, wide eyes, and thin black hair combed over in waves that crash just before his ear.

James enters Tom's office.

"Sir?" says James.

"Sit down Cleary."

James makes sure the rest of his shirt is tucked into his pants before sitting down in the chair. He starts to sweat already.

"You know, we all have put up with you and your dozing off in fantasy land for quite some time James. The leaders are starting to rethink your position here."

"Gosh. I'm sorry," James says. "Please forgive me. I haven't been sleeping lately. The hours- I- I'm not trying to be ungrateful but- maybe I could get more... pay?"

James grits his teeth.

Tom grunts and maneuvers himself in his chair. "You know, you have a lot of nerve asking me for a raise while I'm supposed to be reprimanding you for being lazy."

They stare at each other in silence for a moment. Tom looks him up and down.

"You show up next week and complete your tasks on time. Then, well talk about upping your PC."

Just then, a voice comes over the loudspeaker. "Attention managers, please find your positions. Leadership will be arriving shortly."

James looks out the window and sees three dark green tanks approaching the workplace from the gravel roads. Each tank wears a driver at the front, a gunman on the top and a rider on the back.

The gunmen are known to be tremendous marksmen. They operate the turrets with what seemed to contain endless amounts of ammunition. The riders on the back are always new to leadership positions, but if they held steady maybe, just maybe, one day, they could be a driver.

BOOM

The door busts open, and 15 Leadership members pile into The Workplace. With their guns at the ready, they form a line and move systematically down the hallway passing James and Tom as they are frozen in fear. They stop at the third door on the left side.

"One… two… three…" they count before smashing in the door and shooting various rounds of ammunition into the ceiling.

"Wha-what do we do?" James whispers.

"Nothing. Let them do what they need to do," Tom replies.

Screaming sounds from the room.

At that moment, leadership members drag a man from the office down the hallway. He is unconscious and bleeding from his face, his limp body slides heavily along the tile floor.

"Get back to work!" one of them shouts.

James and Tom disperse along with the rest of the onlookers in the building into their respective offices. James has seen a few of these routines before but it always feels like the first time. His heart is practically jumping from his chest. He gait is as stiff as a board. Sweat droplets drip from his brow. He doesn't understand how everyone else can be so calm.

The Workplace is an extremely large, immaculately white, and wildly impressive building. It was designed and constructed as a huge white cube with sharp and thick edges on every corner. There are fifty-two floors, housing over five thousand people. Every floor looks precisely the same. There is a large square lobby with east and west wings containing most of the Leadership offices. Smaller cubicle-like stations sit just outside of these major offices. These stations are for the less important workers, new hires, interns. That's where James sits as he sweats through his trousers.

A few hours later, The Workplace begins to empty. It's Friday, and everyone is eager to return home in anticipation of The Weekend Rally. James grabs his hat and coat and blends in with the crowd as they scuttle down the steps and into the street. The winter wind blows in every direction, as the trees shiver with no leaves to bare them cover. It is cold and grey. The sun on its last legs.

On Friday, New Haven men go to The Palace on their way home from work. This is where all the built-up tension accrued during the week would be released. Friday is pay day, and in New Haven, there's only one way anyone wants to spend it.

James looks forward to The Palace, almost more than going home to Sybil. She had been so distant lately, which worried James gravely. If leadership would find out, that would certainly be the end of not only his marriage but his way. Being branded a traitor in New Haven is no small thing.

No one could definitively say what they do with such traitors, all James knows, is that once you upset Leadership, you are labeled and that is it. You are fairy dust.

After all, Leadership has provided everything any ordinary man could ever want or need to maintain a healthy relationship with his wife. He should have children, many children, and lead a happy and fulfilled life, knowing that Leadership has his best interest at heart.

Anything to the contrary is tomfoolery and clearly mental illness. There is no mental illness at New Haven; Leadership has fixed all of that. There is only bliss; innocent, complacent, and admittingly sometimes bewildering bliss.

James approaches his regiment-provided shuttle and shows his PC to the card reader. The card reader is skinny as a pin, especially in comparison to the monstrous shuttle apparatus behind it. Each regiment designed shuttle is twenty-two feet tall and eighteen feet wide. It can fit a family of four comfortably as the inside is lavish with charcoal leather heated seating and sporty table trays. The outside of the shuttle is mat-black from nose to butt. The black paint is so dark it absorbs any light that dare touch its surface.

James enters and the shuttle doors closed behind him. Shuttle 1-256 takes off from the workplace straight up into the air like a mini rocket. It is much easier to fly to your destination than it is to sit in traffic with the poor plebs. Afterall, James isn't very keen to be seen around the plebs as they envy him and his position tirelessly.

James was a poor pleb once. He knows what it is like to drown daily in debt. The Plebs aren't allowed person cards and are in complete control of their own finances and jobs. They live the Way but have much less opportunities and privileges than a Workplace worker. The Regiment uses the plebs as an example to show what happens when they don't intervene. They're a constant reminder of the past and why The Way is good, and it *is* good. James remembers his days as a pleb and wishes not to return under any circumstances to that way of life.

James remembers a time when quarters went a long way. He would go to the corner store and buy his mom a pack of cigarettes and use the left-over change that she gave him on a chocolate bar. They didn't have much growing up. James was raised on less than minimum wage and when The Regiment took over, even less. His house smelled of fish and mayonnaise as cans of tuna would feed his family for weeks. The scent stuck to the walls. Respiratory viruses and bacterial infections ran rampant in his neighborhood. House to house. Plebs don't have access to high quality healthcare as medical doctors are only for Leadership. Middle Docs with very limited medical training were cheaper. They are for plebs. For them, every day is a constant battle to survive.

He looks down from the shuttle at the bumper-to-bumper traffic the plebs are forced to endure. Hundreds of gasoline cars stand idlily in a line down two lanes of broken-down roads. The Regiment never provides lane or highway construction for the plebs. But of course, they are free to figure that out on their own if they could afford it. For now, potholes and unevenly paved gravel dominates the streets. Jobs for plebs pay pennies, and public housing costs are in dollars. It's impossible to keep up.

The shuttle speeds through the air until it reaches James's destination, the Palace. The shuttle alights on the landing pad and James makes his way down the stairs and into the lobby. He opens the doors and revels at the stunning architecture of the building. Chandeliers with too many diamonds to count parade the ceilings. Their bright lights radiate all the way down the street and into the sewer dwellings of the plebs. A generously wide and open space, the lobby features three spiral staircases that lead to vast hallways decorated with diamonds and gold. One on the left, one on the right and one down the middle. The world's most beautiful women stroll the floors of the lobby holding trays of champagne and dressed only in skimpy thread like clothing.

James grabs a glass from one of the hostesses and makes his way to the middle staircase. He climbs the rungs, gliding his left hand along the railing and gripping his drink with his right. He stops at the selection chamber and steps into his assigned booth. He scans his PC and relaxes as a robotic arm places vision goggles directly over his eyes.

Here, in this booth, he would "try on" different Worker Women. He could feel the way each of their lips would touch his skin, or anything else he had in mind. He could watch them dance, and even flirt with them in simulated conversations until one would tickle his fancy.

James makes his selection and customizes his experience to his liking. He scans his PC and buckles his chair-belt. The floor of the booth opens outward, and his chair takes him down through a series of tunnels to his selected Worker Women's room where she is waiting for him, ready to perform.

James chooses Mira, a twenty something year old Finnish woman new to New Haven. Mira is naturally beautiful. She has a perfectly symmetrical face with high cheekbones, and full lips. Her skin is buttery smooth and clear. Practically glowing. She has striking, bright green eyes with long lashes and well-groomed eyebrows. Her dark hair is thick, shiny, and perfectly styled, framing her face in the most flattering way. Mira is tall and slender with long legs and a great body. Her posture is graceful but poised, giving her an air of confidence and elegance. She is a primary selection by The Regiment.

In New Haven, it's considered an honor to be chosen as a Worker Woman by the Regiment. The Way ensures it to be considered one of the more noble professions. Only the most beautiful can claim the title as Worker Woman. They have to undergo vigorous checks and training by The Regiment to secure this position. Afterall, they are paid quite generously and are afforded luxurious lifestyles to their fitting. They only work on Fridays.

The Regiment requires Mira to maintain a certain number of Value Points, or VPs, to keep her position at The Palace. If she loses enough value points, she could be downgraded to a bottle girl or kicked out of The Palace entirely. That is ultimately up to leadership, but Mira would never let it get that far. She's good, and always knows how to listen to what her men want. Most of the time, it's just an end of the day blowjob after all.

"There's my man," says Mira as she meets James in the chamber.

"You're looking fabulous. As always," he replies.

"So, what is it today? The usual?"

"The usual."

Mira straddles James in his seat. She looks down at him and meets his gaze as cheesy instrumental music starts to play in the background. The song has no words.

"My heart is racing," James says, laughing to break the tension.

"So is mine," she replies as she runs her hand down his chest.

"I don't want you to be gentle," James says, grabbing her hand with force.

Mira cracks a smile.

"I want you to close your eyes and open them only when I've blown your mind," she says, bending backwards on top of him. Her hands roaming freely as she explores his body.

Two minutes pass. Then, James opens his eyes.

***

He arrives home to find Sybil waiting on him. Sybil is a short gal and has black glasses that chronically rest on the bridge of her nose. Her thick black hair is tied tight behind her head and her work uniform is as tidy and neat as it was when she left the house earlier to work her job at The Fund.

The Fund is the centralized bank where all PCs are linked to. They handle every citizen's income from work, their distribution of funds to various bills and utilities set and designed by The Regiment as well as general data entry tasks. Sybil has been working at The Fund now for 8 years and has earned several privileges from Leadership. These include PC raises, beauty product boxes and a subscription to the most coveted service for Public Women: The Nerve.

Sybil and James's relationship has been rocky for quite some time but especially over the last few months. James is growing tired of Sybils attachment issues and finds her clinginess a nuisance. Sybil is beginning to resent James for his lack of emotional capacity to meaningfully participate in their marriage.

"James, can you not at least look at me when you come in the door?" Sybil shoots.

"I'm sorry honey, it's been a long day at work." I've got to start keeping my focus more, or else we'll be plebs by tomorrow."

"Did you not have your Palace appointment today?" she banters. "I thought that was supposed to focus you."

"Yes, dear," he says. His eyes drooping from fatigue. "I feel great. What is it that you want from me?"

Sybil throws her hands up in the air with frustration. She has heard this expression from James many times before and did not feel particularly interested in explaining her desires for the one thousandth time to her husband. Why can't he just care?

"Alright James. Fine," she says with haste as she marches out the room.

Sybil enters the entertainment room and scans her PC to her VR system. Big bold black letters appear on the screen: **THE NERVE**.

She puts on her Regiment-issued virtual reality goggles and headphones and enters the virtual environment with her beloved Cam waiting for her.

Cam is a Worker Man but not at The Workplace. He works at The Nerve which is kind of like The Palace but for the female sex.

The Nerve is designed to give unfulfilled women what they desperately desire. The selection process for a Worker Man is just as rigorous as the Worker Women. You must be immeasurably attractive and pass all the prerequisite testing performed by The Regiment. This is to make sure you could be trained to give the women clients everything that they desire in a male companion. Once those boxes are checked, Worker Men sign indelible contracts with the husbands of their clients regarding a prophylactic settlement fee.

The settlement fees are in the contracts just in case the Worker Man decides to run off with one of his clients. Should Cam and Sybil fall in love, The Regiment backed contract states that $250,000 from Cams PC would be transferred directly to James's PC balance immediately and without question or trial. This $250,000 had been agreed upon a year ago when Sybil first engaged in the selection process and chose Cam.

Cam is 19 and grew up in a traditional New Haven household. He is the oldest of five brothers and sisters and has a stocky, athletic build. He was every girl's dream in primary school, and everyone knew he would eventually end up at The Nerve. He is quite robotic but has the ability to display an entirely different side of him that oozes charisma when with clients. He is blessed with intense listening skills and an agreeable nature that could make any woman comfortable in his presence.

Cam appears in front of Sybil virtually. They are at their favorite beach at sunset. With a blanket and picnic basket. No one around but them. The magical sound of the ocean tide ebbs and flows. In and out.

"What's wrong baby?" Cam asks, sensing Sybil's frustration.

"I'm not sure anymore," Sybil replies. "I just feel like I'm dreaming. Like I'm always fucking dreaming. Like everything in my life is a blur," she says. Her voice ramping up with intensity.

"I go to work, I come home. I don't even know who I am anymore. I can't believe my fucking husband doesn't even look at me! Like how long can I go-"

"Baby, baby, no," Cam pleads.

His hands run through her hair like endless droves of woven silk. She could feel his touch, as if he is really there. So calming, so nurturing, so necessary.

"It's ok to feel this way you know. He's a dick. You deserve so much better."

The words flow out of him like melted butter.

Sybil smiles as she wipes a tear from her eye. "Why couldn't we have met under normal circumstances?"

She can feel her mood swiftly changing from one of frustration, to one of comfort. At last, for the first time today, she feels safe.

A loud crash rips Sybil away from the moment. The sound comes from outside the house. James rushes to the window at the front door to see what is causing the commotion.

Leadership is arriving in tanks as they surround the house. James quickly flees to the kitchen to dispose of any paraphernalia that leadership might find unacceptable. Watches, gold, jewelry. Anything of monetary value that isn't issued by The Regiment is strictly prohibited.

Sybil flies into the kitchen to find James, rummaging through the kitchen drawers.

"How long do we have?" she asks.

"Seconds, darling," James replies. "Seconds."

The door bursts open, and two Leadership members make their way into James and Sybils modest home.

"Hands! Hands where we can see them!" one of them yells.

"Don't move a fucking muscle until I tell you to," the other says.

James and Sybil shoot their hands into the air. Every finger on both of their hands grips tightly on bills of cash, gold pendants and jewelry. Paraphernalia from their family's old life in Manhattan.

Leadership firearms and flashlights point directly into James and Sybils eyes, blinding them until a voice appears from the doorway.

In walks another Leadership member. This is a short and stubby man with greying hair. A protruding stomach bulks out of his crisp white leadership uniform. His name plate reads: **Matthews - Leadership Division 1**.

Matthews motions over to the other two leadership members to close the door. He takes off his hat at the door and tells James and Sybil to put their hands down, relax, and meet him at the table.

"I come into your house like this for one of two reasons," he says as he moves to his seat. "Either you've done something good, or" he pauses as he sits forward in his chair. "You've done something bad," he says as a smile appears on his tired and overdrawn face. "Which do you believe it is today?" he asks James as though expecting James's response to be a part of his game.

James stutters, "Uh, sir- you see, I- I'm not entirely sure if I'm honest. You see, I've lived The Way, I really have!" He stammers.

Sybil stays quiet. She thinks that any contribution would only lead to a worsened sentence.

"Well, if I were here for what's currently in your hands, you'd both be dust by now," he says with a light chuckle. "No, no, no, today we are here to commend a good man!" Mathews announces to the room as he pounds the table and stands up.

James looks over in Sybil's direction. She stares straight ahead.

"You see, James, the information you provided us last week happened to be a key piece in stopping a war! Your assignment," he said pointing straight at James's chest, "lead to the capture of twenty-five traitors and terrorists that were living among us. Right underneath our very noses!" he said as he taps James's nose. James relaxes his shoulders and releases the air he had been holding hostage in his chest.

"I'll drink to that my good man," Mathews says as he hands James an empty glass from the bar cart.

James smiles and holds the glass awkwardly without moving. Sybil takes it from James and goes to pour some liquor for the men; all the while trying to figure out what exactly is going on.

"Oh, uh- thank you- sir," James rambles. "I-"

"But it seems we do have a problem here after all," Mathews says as he receives his drink from Sybil. "I'm afraid I've noticed quite a bit of paraphernalia in here. That's a big no-no," he says, as he shakes his finger at James back and forth and sips his drink. He retrieves a tablet-like device from his pocket and pulls up James's tracking information.

He strokes his beard as he reads quietly. "Hmm. Are you not satisfied with your life here in New Haven?" Mathew's askes as though truly curious. He continues scanning the pages of information from the screen in front of his face.

"Oh yes. I have all I could ever ask for sir," James replies.

You seem to have a generous monthly stipend from The Workplace on your PC," Mathews says.

"You seem to enjoy The Palace and all of its amenities," he teases.

James bites his lip.

"You have taken the shuttle thirty-six times this month without paying a bill for gas. You live here in this home without paying rent, you have meals provided three times per day," he pauses to take a breath. "I'm troubled James. Enlighten me. What could be so bothersome about this arrangement that would lead you to risk it all for some worthless jewelry and old bills from a land that ceases to exist?"

James's mouth opens slightly but no words come out. He can't seem to figure out exactly just how much trouble he's in. He tries to maintain his composure as he carefully choses his answer.

James sucks in a deep breath. "No, Sir. Not at all. We are perfectly content with what you and The Regiment have provided. These artifacts are just memories you see, memories of where we came from."

Matthews's scowl turns into a faint grin. He enjoys watching people squirm and basks in his privilege to abuse power. He knows James is full of shit but enjoys playing the game so much he will continue to entertain it.

Matthews picks up a piece of jewelry from the table that had been given to Sybil by her late mother. It's a golden locket with a picture inside of a metal heart. A picture that Sybil holds dear as it is the last remaining evidence of her mother's existence.

"You know, memories are an important part of history. They're how we grow and learn from experiences. Wouldn't you agree, Sybil?" he asks, dangling the locket in front of her nose.

She remains silent and still as she feels something bad is about to happen.

"In fact," Matthews continues, "memories are so very important that I think we should always be making new ones. Yes, I am going to help you all with that today. I am going to give us all a new memory so that we can all learn and grow together, like a good community should!"

Matthews walks over to the living room with the locket in hand and more of the paraphernalia in his pocket. He leans over to the fireplace which holds embers of a fire that was recently lit and tosses the locket on top of the burning wood.

Mathews pauses as he stares at the locket, watching it singe. "Memories can be like fire Sybil. They can burn with intensity. They can reach tall heights in your mind and dance until the nights end. They can become quite distracting though. You see, some even say you can see the future in a flame. You just have to look hard enough," he says leaning closer to the fire.

The fireplace embers start to consume the locket.

What future do you see now Sybil? Hmm?" he asks.

Sybil remains silent.

Matthews pulls out his six-shot revolver and waves it crazily in the air. He points it at the fireplace and fires two consecutive shots as ashes explode all over the room. James jumps back with fright. Sybil doesn't move. The two other members of Leadership draw their pistols and point them at James and Sybil.

Matthews throws the rest of the paraphernalia into the now roaring fire. All of James and Sybils savings, gone in an instant.

Matthews appears from the smoke and ashes and dusts off his uniform.

"Great work, James," he says as he places his arm around James's shoulder and leads him back to the kitchen area. "I should turn you to dust you know," he snarls. "But you're just so damn good at your job! Sit down," he says to James as he leads with his revolver before tucking it away in his holster.

Matthews takes another sip from his cup. "We found these two kids James. Twelve and fourteen or something. Hiding in a fucking trap door," he says, bursting with laughter. "They sang the names of traitors like those beautiful canaries you hear about and because of them, I'm going to let you live. In fact, I'm going to let you keep your job and your privileges as it were. That's just how nice I am. Right James?"

James thinks back to some intel he had given Tom a few weeks back. He thought he had discovered an escape operation but was never able to follow up on it. Could he really have finally nabbed some traitors?

"Yes sir, thank you sir," says James. "I'm sorry to have had paraphernalia sir. It won't happen again. You can bet on that."

"Oh, I know it won't," says Matthews. "I'm very sure of it." Matthews turns from the table to the two other leadership members still standing by the door. He takes the last gulp of his drink before slamming the glass down on the table.

"Proxy for a month," he demands as he walks out the door and back to his vehicle.

James hangs his head.

Being assigned a proxy means that a Leadership member will be moving into their home and living with them for a predetermined amount of time. The proxy is responsible for making sure that James and Sybil have everything that they need to live The Way properly. The proxy is instructed to teach James and Sybil to live good. And it is good. To rid them of things that might influence them away from the proper way of life. To keep them well within the ranks of public society and not let them falter into treasonous or traitorous activities that might have them straying further from the path.

The good path. And it *is* a good path

2 PROXY

DING. DING. DING.

The shrill alarm bell wrenches James from sleep at 5am. He opens his eyes briefly to a haze.

DING. DING. DING.

He closes his eyes once more in an effort to possibly absorb a single more minute of sleep as he dreads the day ahead. No such luck—the Proxy bursts through his bedroom door.

"Time to move James. Up and at 'em," the Proxy commands.

James groans and stands at the foot of his bed awaiting instruction. He realizes Sybil is absent. He can feel his eyes wanting to shut again as he slept not longer than 30 minutes the entire night. He stares directly ahead as the Proxy moves in front of him.

"Your schedule today is as follows. At 5:30 you will enjoy morning Green Grass along with your wife. At 6:00, we will shuttle to the field. We will attend the weekend rally until 3pm. At precisely 3pm, we will eat our lunch which is graciously provided by the Regiment. Then we will return to home base. At home base, you will receive further instruction. Is that clear?"

"Crystal," says James standing straight as an arrow. He feels like rolling his eyes but refrains.

"Get dressed for the rally," says the proxy as he abruptly leaves the room.

James meets Sybil in the hallway. She's an early riser. They exchange glances which convey more than if they had opened their mouths.

The Proxy pours them Green Grass as James and Sybil take their seats at the breakfast table. Regiment approved reading paper is provided for James, as Sybil sips her drink. James opens the paper to a great big and bold headline.

25 TRAITORS TO BE FLUSHED TODAY AT THE RALLY. HEROS WELCOME.

As James begins to read the story under the headline, he notices his name in print.

Thanks to the heroes at the workplace under the supervision of James Cleary, a plot involving 25 traitors was quashed. James and his crew will be honored at today's rally for their efforts in keeping New Haven great.

James sits back in his chair and shoots Sybil a look of uncertainty. She returns his gaze as she receives a teaspoon from the Proxy.

"Drink up! We should try not to be late," the Proxy barks.

James and Sybil sip their drinks slowly, trying not to alter their facial expressions as the Green Grass is known to have a strong and bitter taste. No one knows exactly what is in it, but it is Regiment-approved. And it *is* good for you. Packed with substances in a regiment facility just on the border of New Haven and the neighboring faction Brightwater, James had heard rumors of what the contents of the Green Grass might actually be. One former co-worker of James had told him that it contained a chemical called Lieber. One of the newest man-made scientific innovations that was concocted to make the general public more agreeable and tamer in nature. One rumor, floated around the idea that it contains the blood of traitors and that's why it tastes so metallic. While the ingredients were unknown in truth, the one thing that is for sure, is that Green Grass must be your morning brew today, tomorrow, and every day thereafter until no more days are left.

James, Sybil, and the Proxy shuffle into the shuttle and take off toward the weekend rally. Their short journey is silent as the three of them spend the time staring out the window at the vast areas of land and grey space. Sybil looks down and notices groups of people between swaths of grey buildings. They resemble ants in a colony. Moving around with goals and directives. Trying not to get eaten. Servicing the queen.

They land just outside of the grounds as citizens begin to make their way into the event. James exits the shuttle, realizing this rally is far bigger and more extravagant than any of the weekend rallies he had previously attended.

Countless red, white, and black banners displaying The Regiment symbol of an axe, fly as high as the sky. Fighter planes and rockets advance overhead at frightening speeds. Tanks surround the encampment, with the barrels of their blasters pointing straight into the air, as if to aim at the gods themselves. Members of Leadership march in unison in various formations around the compound. It immediately becomes easy to feel lost or out of place. The sheer magnitude of this event quickly becomes intimidating as James and Sybil make their way amongst the rest of the crowd with the Proxy tightly in tow.

With the Leadership led marching bands playing the New Haven fight song, a large circle begins to form around a centralized stage that hosts solely a podium and a microphone.

The entire crowd sings together.

Blessed are we who fight for peace.
Fight the bastards to their knees.
We live for you, and you live for me.
In New- Hay---Ven! Hey! Hey!

The music begins to build to a final crescendo when a large rocket, nearly three times the size of James's shuttle 1-256, appears from the clouds overhead. It slowly makes its descent toward the stage as enormous flames of fire become visible from the rocket's boosters. The entire crowd looks up and simultaneously shielding their vision from the bright lights of the flames that ferociously approach them. The rocket lands smoothly on a pad next to the stage as members of leadership form a line in front of the door to welcome whoever was behind it.

The door flies open, and a figure begins to appear through the smoke of the doorway. A tall and overweight blonde woman appears, donning a red pantsuit and colorful glasses. She wears crisp white high heels with sharp points at the end and sports large black diamond earrings which dangle heavily from each earlobe. She walks with conviction down the line of leadership members toward the podium as the crowd of thousands roars with applause.

James and Sybil have never seen this woman before. But everyone in New Haven knows she's important.

"Good morning New Haven!" she exclaims into the mic as the crowd responds with cheers and applause. "Welcome to this very, very special weekend rally. Today is not just about supporting the great leadership that helps New Haven run so smoothly. Today is going to be about you!" she says as she points into the vast crowd of people. "Today is a great lesson and example, as to how leadership and The Way are good. And they are good. Today will exemplify what true society looks like and what it can be, when everyone cooperates toward the common goal."

The woman speaks with such passion, it's as if a fire has been lit under her arse and is burning as bright as the boosters on her rocket.

"Thanks to leadership and the regiment," she says as she motions her hand over to leadership members standing next to the stage, "we have created a system where the general public can thrive! James Cleary is such an example."

James's heart drops.

"Mr. Cleary, under direct supervision of Leadership, led a task force of men at the workplace to uncover a group of terrorists plotting to overthrow our great nation," she says fervently. "Mr. Cleary and his team uncovered twenty-five motherfuckers, that don't enjoy the eutopia that we have provided. So today, we will all take effort together, to flush these cockroaches into oblivion."

The crowd roars and chants break out.

"Flush those fucks! Flush those fucks! Flush those fucks!"

In an effort to fit in, James raises his fist and joins in the chant. He grabs Sybil's arm, forcing it in the air as the Proxy watches closely behind them.

"It is finally time to face judgement! Leaders of the prime division, show us the traitors!" she screams, as every eyeball in the crowd shifts to the right of the stage where five large objects are covered by an even larger tarp. The leadership members pull on the tarp revealing the twenty-five traitors all bound and tied to a stake. They are stripped of their clothing and appear filthy from days and nights in captivity by the regiment. Boos vibrate the air from various subsections of the crowd. The traitors are shamed and humiliated.

"We will begin the flushing ceremony today, starting with the heroes that helped uncover this plot. James Cleary and his crew, please approach the stage to take part in this glorious ceremony."

James's heart drops as he begins to sweat through his collared shirt and trousers. He glances at Sybil, but she's pale providing very limited reassurance. The proxy proceeds to escort James through the vast crowd of people. They are cheering loudly, chanting his name and for just a split second, he feels a sense of true belonging. For so long, he was just a man at the workplace. For so long, he went disregarded by his peers. For so long he felt worthless. But today he is the hero. And that feels good.

As he makes his way through the innumerable amount of people, he looks up at the traitors on the stage. Twenty-five faces, all men, look back at him with intense fear. They have no idea what he will do to them, and James doesn't either. All he can conceive at this point is that he is now the punisher instead of the punished.

As James gets closer to the steps of the stage, he recognizes one of the faces. His childhood friend, Charlie, whom James hadn't seen in over ten years. The thrill that has just flushed through James, now abandoned him completely.

Charlie? A traitor?

Charlie and James grew up together in a poor pleb neighborhood smack dab in the middle of New Haven and were inseparable during their time as neighbors. They often slept over at each other's houses staying up all night dreaming up big schemes about how they would make their way into the general public and become important people. James and Charlie spent so much time together that their parents soon became good friends, and they would spend nearly every holiday together; tied at the hip. Now it seemed that friendship would find its end, as Charlie is bound, gagged, and sentenced, facing a most uncertain future.

James arrives at the top step of the stage and awaits instruction as the beaming sun in the sky warms his face. His crew members from the workplace are forming a line behind him. Seven or eight young men all nervous smiles, all excited at the opportunity to be recognized on a stage as large as this. All naive, with no idea what is to come next. James fiddles with his hands as the collective nervous energy becomes abundant.

The Woman motions for them to come up close to her and she receives them with open arms. She grabs James's hand, forcing it into the air like he had just done with Sybil. The crowd lets out a thunderous roar, as the gravity of the situation begins to show its face. James forces a smile as he looks out at the vast crowd of people. Being recognized feels good for James. He feels heroic. But he can't stop thinking about Charlie.

There's no way he was involved in this. He would never.

The Woman receives a long black square case from her assistant and rests it on the podium. She clicks the two locks of the case forward to open it, slowly revealing its contents. A twenty-seven-inch silver sword that glimmers with beauty. It lay firmly in its case. She lifts the sword by the handle and inspects it in front of the crowd. There is a tense aura spreading throughout the event that infects every person in attendance as they are all waiting to see what will happen next. She holds the sword in her right hand and drops it by her side to demonstrate its weight as she walks over to where the prisoners are bound. She stops before a boy no older than fourteen and displays the sword. His mouth is gagged, and his hands are tied, but his eyes grow as wide as the room as he knows he is looking at pain.

"Traitors cannot be tolerated in New Haven," she states to the crowd as she turns to the boy. "You knew that; didn't you?"

The boy nods and starts to whimper through the cloth that gags his voice.

"Now you must be punished." She draws the sword close to his throat. She places the blade horizontally across his larynx and makes a small incision. It's enough to illicit pain and a few drops of blood, but the boy will live.

"And how was that for treason?" The Woman asks the crowd facetiously.

The crowd boos and hisses, demonstrating their disapproval with the leniency of her selected punishment.

A grin appears on the Woman's face after this reception from the crowd. She is permitted to advance further. She goes back again with the sword but this time, it is over the young man's crotch.

"Is this what you want?" she asks the crowd in jest.

They respond louder than ever with cheers and applause. She looks the young boy in his pale blue eyes and whispers, "You won't be needing these," and slices with ferocity through the young boy's scrotum, spilling his testicles and their contents onto the floor.

The boy screams in agonizing pain, but his muffled howls are drowned out by the noise of the building and the gag in his mouth. As he begins to hemorrhage, the Woman motions over for her assistant to bring out a second object, a large round and unlabeled blue bucket. She places the bucket underneath the poor boy's pelvis to catch all the blood that poured from his genitals as the young boy's body becomes limp.

James watches this in terror, entirely unsure of his role up on that stage. Every red blood cell in his body shoots to his brain as the rest of his body turns ghost white. He has never seen this kind of ruthless corporal punishment. The Woman calls James over and asks him to assist with the next prisoner to which he hopelessly obliges. She spins the stake that holds the prisoners clockwise to reveal the next to be punished, Charlie.

James stares into Charlie's eyes and wishes this was a nightmare from which he would soon wake. Charlie stares back at James in utter disbelief, as he begins to recognize his old pal standing in front of him. This seems to elicit a glimmer of hope that somehow, Charlie might just get out of this. James can see the helpless pleading coming from Charlie's eyes. As if he was asking James to just bail him out this one time. But how could he?

I'm surrounded by thousands of people that want to see me commit whatever egregious act I'm about to be asked to do and they'll likely kill me if I refuse. I don't see a way out of this.

The Woman hands the sword to James with blood still on the blade and instructs him to punish the prisoner.

"Punish him!" she exclaims! "Show him what it means to be a cockroach traitor," she says as she positions herself to motion to the crowd. James holds the sword for a few seconds as he considered the options for his next action. He could swing it at the Woman, but he'd surely end up dead from the rest of leadership that surrounds the stage. He could try to make an excuse as to why he could not complete his instruction which would make him appear sympathetic to treason. Or he could swing the sword as quickly and lethally as he could, with intent to give his old friend a quick and painless death. James makes his decision and raises the sword above his head. Charlie closes his eyes as he can tell that his time on this earth was limited to seconds. James quivers with the sword raised high, knowing that his only option is to kill his friend with a frightful blow. He closes his eyes, twists the sword as he lifts it higher and slices directly across Charlie's neck as fast and as hard as he can muster. Charlie's head falls to the floor below his body and takes one small bounce as blood spurts directly into the air. The crowd roars as The Woman's assistant places another bucket to where the blood spills. James breaks, his mind silently screaming.

He stands in one singular position as all the noise in the building becomes deafening. Dazed, he thinks about what he had just done. The sword is taken out of his hand and placed in the hand of another. As James steps aside and everyone on stage drains blood from the traitors, James's worldview crumbles. Moments blur together into one entirely horrible afternoon.

After the twenty-five traitors are executed and various blue buckets become full, the Woman starts to hand them out to various members of the crowd before returning to the microphone.

"This has been a joyous and fruitful occasion that we have all celebrated here today," she states. "But there is still one thing left to do. We will now wash our hands with the blood of the traitors so that this experience will be imprinted into our DNA. Everyone will place their hands in one of the buckets so that each palm is colored entirely red and then you will shake hands with your neighbor to show your understanding of the rules and regulations of New Haven." Countless blue buckets circulate throughout the crowd, and thousands of people do as the Woman commands. The blood of the traitors flows over the citizens and members of Leadership. They have devoured the enemy and are now basking in its defeat.

***

James's scheduled lunch takes place at 3pm exactly. He sits down at a wooden picnic table outside of the event grounds with Sybil sitting across from him, silent. James is numb. They are each provided a turkey sandwich and a glass of milk. As James unwraps his sandwich in front of The Proxy, three members of leadership approach his table. He takes a quick bite and places the sandwich back down as they appear directly behind Sybil.

"Mr. Cleary" one of them announces. My name is Barlow. I am part of security detail for senior Leadership members. You're going to need to come with us."

James lets out a long sigh before standing up and following Barlow 50 yards to a war tent set up behind the venue. He is exhausted. James can hardly gather his thoughts as he struggles to keep up with time. He moves his gaze upward and looks at the sky. It's clear. Beautiful white clouds float overhead without a hint of precipitation.

I wish the day was as nice as the sky looks right now.

As they approach the tent, James's daydream is interrupted by voices. The Woman is standing over a table that displays a hologram of the surrounding landscape as well as vast areas of land that James cannot immediately recognize. As James enters the tent with Barlow, The Woman halts her discussions with the tight group of leadership members and dismisses them from the tent.

"That will be all," she says to Barlow, motioning for him to leave as well. "James, come join me at the vision board." She urges him to get a closer look at the floating, holographic images.

"Woah" James exclaims as he starts to get a better look at the images. "What's with all of the red dots?"

"Immediately asking questions. I like that about you James," says The Woman with a light chuckle. "I like how you're not afraid to say what you think and ask for what you want."

James nods with his eyes fixed on the numerous red pulsating dots on the hologram map.

"What do you want?" she asks.

James stops for a second to think about the question.

Is this a test? Is there a wrong answer here? One that will get me turned to dust. What does she want?

"Erm, well, I guess, I just want to be happy," he says sincerely, hoping she will see this as a good answer.

"So, does that mean you are not happy?" the Woman asks sharply. "Does your wife make you happy? What about New Haven? Does The Palace make you happy? Enlighten me James, I'm quite curious."

Tension grows as silent seconds pass.

"Yeah," James mumbles unconvincingly. "Yeah, no I'm very happy! Sybil is great. You know, every marriage requires work as I'm sure you- uh- yeah, no we're good. Really, were great actually. Uh-"

"James."

"Yes ma'am?"

"I don't like rambling."

"Right, sorry about that," he says, stopping to take a breath. "Sybil and I are perfectly content here. Perfectly content indeed."

The Woman stares at James for a while. Studying him. Watching him squirm in this certainly uncertain situation. She has him by the balls and she knows it.

"James, by now you're probably wondering why I've called you in here and to put it bluntly, I find you very impressive," she says as she moves to the other side of the table. She stands so close to him; he can feel her every breath on his cheek.

"How would you feel about advancing up another rung in the ladder?" she asks him.

James's jaw shows slack.

"If you do well this last couple of weeks with The Proxy, you could be working directly under me," she says with a hint of seduction and flattery.

"Truly, I would be honored!" James quickly replies, entirely unaware of The Woman's flirtatious tone. "Thank you, ma'am!"

"James, we don't do this very often, but I see something in you. I think you would be a fine addition to the leadership team and could help The Regiment do a lot of good. And it would be good. You know, we could even get you a new wife, if you found this one to be, unsuitable," she says.

"Uh- please- forgive me- but doesn't The Regiment always preach how we should have a good marriage with our wife and that there is no reason to argue and fight because The Regiment has provided everything that we need to have a good and happy life? Isn't that the whole-"

"James," she interjects. "When you are a part of leadership, you, live by a- different way let's call it. You abide by a different set of rules you see. The Way as it's taught, is really meant to guide the general public because they don't know better; and how could they. They don't have the tools necessary to understand what a true community needs to be successful. and happy," she emphasizes. "You, on the other hand are special James. You seem to understand this well. I think you will do splendid in your new position."

She rests her hand on James's shoulder.

James glances over at her hand on his shoulder and his eyes slowly make direct contact with hers.

Is she hitting on me right now?

"What do you say, James?" She brings her face closer to his. They are inches apart now, breathing the same air. He thinks about what she had made him do to those prisoners just hours earlier. How sick it makes him feel. How he was forced to put an end to his childhood friend's life at the hand of a cursed blade. Rage starts to consume him.

She places her lips an inch from his. The prospect of joining leadership and climbing the ranks floods his mind as it is intriguing after all. It tugs on his true desires to be noticed, to be relevant. He feels like if he could just put his rage aside, he could use this new opportunity to do some good. He feels like maybe, just maybe, he could find something in this to be proud of which masquerades in flushes of dopamine and serotonin as he leans into her lips.

3 CAMERON

The following Friday, Sybil finds herself home alone while James makes his way to The Palace. She ventures to the entertainment room and logs on to The Nerve impatiently awaiting her virtual sweetheart, Cam.

"Hello, my sweet," Cam says softly. His big burly hands lightly grasp her cheeks. They are deep in the mountains, alone, far away from their lives and in a passionate embrace.

"Hello love," Sybil replies.

She turns her head to the vast landscape that surrounds them. "Isn't this just beautiful?"

They match smiles.

"Speaking of beauty. I've brought you something. But you must promise not to share it. Deal?"

Sybil nods.

Cam retreats to find his backpack in their tent by the fire.

Sybil looks out into the vastness of the canyon below her. The air is thin and crisp. She looks down at the tops of trees and realizes the height of their elevation.

That's a long drop.

Cam returns and pulls out a small black pocket that is tied at the top with some string. Sybil can make out an outline of a square bulge in the pocket prompting her imagination to run wild with possibilities of what the gift might be.

Sybil brings her hand to her mouth as Cam unties the string and pulls out a small jewelry box. He brings it closer to her and looks up and into her eyes before opening the box. There lies an absolutely stunning diamond ring.

"Sybil, you have made me the happiest man in the world."

Cam takes a breath and laughs at his nerves.

I find myself intoxicated by your beauty. You are so smart, and so witty. I never know what to expect from you. You keep me consistently surprised. You deserve so much… more."

Sybil looks away and bites her lip.

"If we can't be together in the real world, we can surely be together in this one. Will you, be mine?"

Tears start to sting Sybil's eyes – mostly joyful tears, but some carry resentment. Resentment for a world where she has to resort to virtual measures to feel complete.

Sybil swallows before speaking. "I am always yours, Cameron. Always yours in this world and the next," she says as she takes the ring. She examines it, finding it pure of any imperfections. The diamonds on the ring reflect brilliantly in the setting sun over the most intensely wonderful landscape of undulating mountains. All colors of the spectrum glisten from her eyes as she melts in the heat of this moment.

He must have saved a lot of money for this.

Sybil places the ring in her jacket pocket which has an item save feature. Anything placed in this pocket will be 3d printed from a Regiment provided printer that is stored in the entertainment room of her home. Any item printed from this machine will also resemble the initial item perfectly, to the point in which they are indistinguishable from each other. It will be ready and waiting for her when she finishes this visit with Cam.

Cam and Sybil spend the next two hours walking in the brilliant mountainous wilderness and roasting marshmallows by the fire. Sybil tells Cam about the events of the weekend rally and how she feels she is losing her connection with James. Cam listens intently as he fiddles with the knots in her hair. It's easy for the two of them to revel in the time they spend together as time itself seems to not exist in their company.

"I want to meet in person," Cam says, as he looks into Sybil's eyes. They are holding each other tightly, eye to eye, skin to skin.

Sybil hesitates and breaks their embrace. "But what if we are caught? I can't bear to think of what they will do to you; to us. You know, James is going to be in leadership now. If he wants you turned to dust, it will happen Cam. I can't bear to lose you."

"I'd risk that for you, Sybil. You speak the words, and I will be there, in person."

Sybil folds her arms together and looks down at the ground.

Silence.

"I want to run away with you Sybil. I- I think we should leave this place, you, and me," he says as he reaches for her hand.

Sybil blushes as she turns from Cam. Adrenaline rushes through her veins.

"Let me put some things together, my love. I just need some time to think this through. I love you. I do. Just give me some time if you would."

Cam looks down in disappointment. Sybil puts her hand under his chin and lifts his gaze up from the ground.

"We will be together love," she whispers. "Just some time."

Sybil takes off her headset and retreats from her experience to the entertainment room of her home. As she reorients herself, she looks at the printer where the diamond ring lies in the dark shadows of the room. Sybil picks up the ring and studies it. She notices an inscription on the side of the ring that reads C & S. She smiles, and as she places the ring in her pocket, the front door opens.

James and The Proxy shuffle into the house escaping the downpour of rain that's pattering above on the tin roof. They wipe their boots at the door as James yells for Sybil.

"Sybil! Sybil!" He yells. "What is for supper darling? I believe I've worked up quite the appetite."

The Proxy makes his way to the kitchen to find a drink as Sybil meets James at the doorway.

"Hello, love," she says as she takes James's coat and places it on the rack.

Sybil notices the proxy's blank but intimidating and expecting expression.

I hate this guy.

What can I cook for you this evening?" she asks politely.

"Oh, must I tell you how to do everything, Woman?" James snaps.

"Oh- We're in a bit of a mood today I see," says Sybil, surprised at his temper. "What is it love, were the ladies at The Palace unimpressed with your performance?"

James raises his eyebrows and puckers his lips. He looks over at the Proxy who is intently listening in on their conversation with squinted eyes and a scowl on his face.

James thinks briefly to himself and assesses the situation. He turns back to Sybil, raises his hand over his head and smacks her violently across the face.

Sybil lurches backwards.

"What the fuck was that, James? What the fu-"

"How dare you insult me in front of The Proxy in our own home!" James screams. "Have you lost your mind, Sybil? Have you gone fucking bananas to think you can speak to me in such a manner?"

James grabs her wrist and drags her to the kitchen. The ring that Cam had just gifted her falls from her pocket, clattering on the floor. James stops dead in his tracks and releases his grip on Sybil's wrist.

James picks up the ring from the ground, inspecting it. "And what is this? What in the name of the good Regiment is this frightful piece?"

"It's nothing!" Sybil exclaims as she tears it from James's hand. "It's a ring I had printed- as a gift!"

"A gift?" James repeats mockingly. "A gift for whom Sybil. Huh? A gift for whom?" He moves closer to her face. "Were you planning on proposing to the queen?"

"I- I was going to give this ring, to- to- The Woman. The Woman from the rally, James! I was making her jewelry to show my appreciation for her leadership and for helping you!" she says pointing directly at James's chest as her voice gets louder and tears stream from her face.

James stands erect and almost expressionless. His arms crossed and head held high. He desperately hopes The Proxy isn't still watching.

"It was a gesture! A nice gesture James, that you are completely spoiling," she says between sniffles. She yanks back the ring and storms into another room before slamming the door.

James stands there silently and brushes his hair back from his face. He turns to face the Proxy. "My apologies sir," he says. "I'm not sure what's gotten into her."

The proxy is seated at the dining table, digesting what he had just seen take place. He takes a sip of his drink before placing his glass back down on the table.

"That was a good effort, James. A good effort indeed. Women can be like this as they often have trouble controlling their emotions. They require us men to remain strong and disciplined. I believe you have done that, so well done. However, this kind of outburst cannot happen as frequently as I believe they do. We will be forced to make changes should this continue."

James stands in silence.

"You are not to tell a soul of this James. You are not to make anyone aware of what goes on in your house that is not me or Leadership. Is that understood?"

"Yes sir. Of course," replies James. "Everything will be worked out in time. I will speak to Sybil later tonight when her hormones have left her. I will have this handled," says James. "With full discretion in mind."

4 LEADERSHIP

3 weeks later

James goes to work on Monday with a confident stride in his step. He ventures through the open doors of the workplace and advances to the slide.

The slide is a more convenient way to get above and below various floors of a building. It is proven to be safer and quicker than a traditional elevator. All one has to do is scan their PC, step into the chamber, and then the slide not only advances to their desired work floor but to the exact location of the surrounding office. It accomplishes this by rising up through the floor panels of a particular room and pushing that floor panel to match with one in the ceiling. Once the destination is reached, James can exit the vessel practically in the middle of a room if he needs to.

James arrives on his new floor, seven, to see his colleagues at their desks, quietly working away. James finds his new corner office with an oversized name plate especially inscribed for him, mounted on the front part of the door. It reads:

James Cleary

Assistant Manager- Section 3E

Intelligence

James grins as he opens the door to find a well sized black desk with three monitors around the seating area. The walls of his office are covered with two-way tempered smart glass. He has a perfect view of the outside workspace and the workers that are working below him. As he looks through the glass at one individual at his desk, the smart glass automatically illuminates in red lighting that can only be seen from the inside. The glass displays the worker's name, age, current assignment, and a workspace grade. He can also have the glass display any other characteristics that he would find useful in evaluating his new staff. When James looks away, the red lighting disappears. When he looks again, it reappears. James repeats this action looking back and forth, giggling to himself at this impressive technology when, suddenly, a knock comes at the door.

"Come in," James says clearing his throat in embarrassment. The door opens and there stands Mathews.

"You know we can see you through that glass right, Cleary?" Mathews asks with a laugh. "It's a nice set up you have here. I think you'll enjoy your own private space as well as I did all those years ago."

"Yes sir, I believe I will," James responds trying to maintain eye contact with Mathews. "I can say, I wasn't expecting to see you here at the workplace. Will I be reporting to you then?" he asks.

"No," says Mathews. "I am here on a special assignment, but you will be reporting to Lester, Leadership division 2. He is your superior. A good man."

"Right," says James. "Very well then."

"Well, I'll let you get back to work now and continue with your... neck exercises. Enjoy your first day and may luck be with you, should you need it," says Mathews as he leaves the doorway and heads out of the facility.

James finds that final comment insidious as he wonders if Mathews is trying to tell him something or just simply pulling his leg. He settles down in his desk, places his briefcase on the floor, and turns on the front monitor. On the screen, he sees what appears to be a biographical profile on a man that he does not recognize. The man's name reads:

Jacob Ferris

Age- 38

Occupation- Labor

Wife- Anita Ferris, 35

Children- 1. Joshua Ferris, 7.

James turns on the second monitor which is stationed to the left of the first one. It displays an active GPS tracing of a person that is identified by only a moving red marker. James hovers the cursor over the red marker showing the initials JF-38.

James figures that he will be tracking this individual for reasons that are currently unknown. However, he feels sure they will soon be revealed.

James turns on the monitor to the right which shows a list of names of both men and women of varying ages and biometric data. He scans the list of names to look for some familiarity but comes up empty as none of them are remotely recognizable. In satisfying his curiosity of his new environment, James begins to rummage through the drawers of his new desk and stops when he comes across a small tablet in the upper right drawer. He picks up the tablet which reveals a small bean-shaped object that is carefully placed behind it. As he picks up the small object, the tablet turns on and displays in big bold letters:

PLACE THE EARPIECE IN YOUR RIGHT EAR JAMES CLEARY.

James stares at the object, bewildered. He places the earpiece in his ear and immediately feels the incomprehensible sensation of complete cancellation of noise. His left ear is open to the environment and can take in and process auditory data; however, his right ear is locked into a digital connection that has no ties to the surrounding noise of the world. It is deathly quiet.

"Hello James," says a grumbly voice over the earpiece. James's pupils dilate like a hit of acid has been dropped on his tongue. The voice in the earpiece is crisp and clear as if it were coming from his own subconscious mind. Devoid of static or interference.

"My name is Lester Prime, it's a pleasure to make your acquaintance.

Silence.

"Somebody seems to like you. I hope you know that. This won't be easy though. I have some expectations for you that I will make clear in time. For now, I want you to settle in as best you can and introduce yourself to everyone in the office."

James remains silent.

"James, hello James? You can speak now," says Lester.

"Oh right, ha, hello sir. It's truly a wonder to meet you as well. Thank you for giving me all of this," he says with appreciation. "Are you really, like, there?" James asks sincerely.

"Am I really there?" replies Lester. Mate, are you joking? Does this sound like the voice of god?" He says laughing through his teeth. "Relax James, it's quite alright. Yes, I am a real person. Yes, we will meet in person eventually. No, I am not omniscient or omnipresent. I am just like you, flesh, blood, and human, but of a slightly higher rank."

James begins to laugh at the silliness of the conversation he is having at the workplace. The mood has never been so nonchalant while conversing with one of his superiors. He wonders if this is what getting respect feels like.

"Right, thank you sir. I look forward to working with you, truly," he says. Trying to appear somewhat professional.

After Lester says goodbye, the line clicks, and James takes off the earpiece and places it back into the drawer. James is full of newfound enthusiasm. He finally feels like he belongs, like he's respected. James's eyes brighten and he stands firm like the important businessman he has always wanted to be. He straightens his collar, tightens his belt, and checks his hair in the mirror before opening the door to his office and making his way over to the other desks outside.

"Hello everyone, if I could have your attention," James announces confidently to the room as he stands outside of his office. "My name is James Cleary, and I am your new superior. It's great to meet all of you and I look forward to building relationships with you all. Now, in the interest of moving forward I would appreciate if each one of you would come, one at a time, into my office and introduce yourselves. James clears his throat. Thanks very much," he says as he retreats back to his desk.

At once, members from the workplace line up outside of his office to greet him. The first is a young man with straight black hair. He has rough eyes but an inviting smile. His skin is taught without blemishes or imperfections. He is tall and classically handsome with heavily accentuated dark features.

"Hello Mr. Cleary," he says as he enters James's office. "My name is Cyrus. Cyrus Bell."

"Great to meet you Cyrus," James replies. "How long have you worked here?" he asks.

"Uh, roughly 3 years sir. I was a promote from the labor camp."

James squints his eyes and turns up his nose.

"I very much enjoy this position sir and I'll do anything to keep it. The Regiment has been so good to us, so good. I only wish to work as hard as they do to keep us well in hand."

James looks at Cyrus intently while he is speaking, studying his face. He enjoys this new power dynamic that burns like fire in his hands. There is something odd about Cyrus though that James can feel down to his core. As James watches Cyrus's lips moving, he gets the impression that he shouldn't trust a single word that escapes from his lips. The hairs on the back of James's neck stand straight as an arrow.

"Very good Cyrus," James responds as he leans forward in his chair. "Very good. It's good to have men like you in the workplace. You know, I, myself am a great believer in hard work and luck. I find that the harder I work, the more luck I seem to find," says James, making direct eye contact. His tone is serious, and he is actively trying to intimidate Cyrus.

"Cyrus, I am not a man that appreciates baseless flattery. I am not a man that finds other men that are incapable of being anything but pedantic, amusing. I am a man that appreciates honest hard work with shoelaces tied tightly." He pauses for a moment to let marinate what he has just communicated to his subordinate.

Cyrus nods slowly pursing his lips.

"Buckle down and find me traitors," says James.

He enjoys giving demands.

Cyrus straightens his back. "Yes sir, I will. I'll get on it straight away."

This continues for the next hour or so as James gets acquainted with the rest of his staff. After he is finished with the introductions, he hears beeping coming from the tablet that is stored in the front drawer. He pulls the tablet out and reads in big bold letters:

JAMES CLEARY INITIATION MEETING 17:35

CONFERENCE FLOOR B15

PLACE EARPIECE DIRECTLY IN LEFT EAR

James squints his eyes and drops his head back in confusion. Mathews and Lester had not mentioned any initiation meeting to him. James shrugs and places the tablet in his briefcase, the earpiece in his ear, stands from his desk, and makes his way to the slide.

Upon arrival, James sees a room full of Leadership members and managers from the workplace ahead of him. They are all seated in front of two glass doors surrounded by freshly painted white walls decorated in leadership achievement awards. He joins the room and sits in one of the available waiting chairs. James is fidgeting in his seat as he waits for something to happen when just then, the two glass doors open automatically, revealing a dark hallway. One by one, the leadership members start to walk down the hallway.

Everyone focuses straight ahead, and no one acknowledges James's presence at all. James struggles internally as he hasn't the slightest clue of what this initiation would entail, but he follows them into the darkness, nonetheless.

As they find the end of the dark hallway, the lights come on abruptly and every single person in the room turns to James and is staring at him. No one says a word. No one blinks an eye.

James jumps back. His eyebrows nearly touch his hairline. He looks around at all the empty faces and eyes that are looking directly at him.

"Uhm, hello?" James says sheepishly. "Someone please tell me what is going on."

James turns behind him to see more blank stares and empty faces looking at him intently.

"Hello!" he says a bit louder. "Why are you all staring at me like this?"

"James Cleary front and center!" booms a voice from a speaker above them.

Just then, the entire crowd forms a circle around him with a single step. All of them still staring into his soul. A spotlight emerges and focuses on James as the rest of the room becomes dark. All James can see are the whites of eyes and teeth of his colleagues that surround him.

There is nowhere to run.

"Turn around James," says the crowd simultaneously in a soft and somber tone. "Turn around James," they repeat at a higher volume. "Turn around James," they repeat again in concert but even louder this time. All of them speaking the exact syllables of the phrase at the same time together in flawless and terrifying harmony.

James turns around and sees the faint outline of a girl, bound, and tied to a wooden chair, her back facing him. She is sitting still.

The Woman then appears from the darkness holding a Regiment designed, powerful handheld firearm which she dangles from her left hand.

"Hello, again my rising star," she says to James. "Welcome, to your initiation ceremony."

James stands in place stunned with fear.

What the hell is this?

He shakes his head and straightens his back trying his best to squeeze out a hint of bravery.

"What's going on? Who is in that chair?" asks James, trying his best to remain calm.

"Oh, well I'm glad you asked James." The Woman swings the chair around with force revealing the prisoner. Sybil.

"Help me, James, please don't do what they are telling you!" Sybil screams as tears flow down her cheeks. "It's a trap!"

James cringes as he sees his wife on the edge of what seems like an inevitable death.

"What is this? What has she done?"

"Sybil was caught smuggling traitors across the border James. She is a good–for–nothing cockroach traitor!" declares The Woman. She hands the firearm to James. "End her. Do as I say and pull the trigger," demands The Woman. "Now."

"No! it's not true!" Sybil begs.

The surrounding crowd starts to jeer in amusement and are all chanting, **"END HER, END HER, END HER, END HER!"**

James looks around at the faces that surround him as they exude hate and ferocity. Their eyes bloodshot red and bulging out of their sockets. The chants get louder.

"END HER, END HER, END HER!"

James gently raises the revolver, pointing it directly at Sybil's forehead.

"END HER, END HER, END HER!"

James looks all around him. Hoping something will happen to interrupt the ceremony. His hand now furiously wobbling as he points the gun.

"DO IT!" The Woman yells. "Do it now!"

James's hands convulse as he looks again at Sybil. "I'm sorry," he mouths to her.

"James, no! Please!" Sybil begs. "Have mercy!"

James lets out a scream, closes his eyes, clenches his teeth tighter, and pulls the trigger three times.

BANG, BANG, BANG.

He gasps for air as he opens his eyes. He finds himself still in his chair, covered in sweat, alone in his office. He pops out of his chair and looks out the glass to see Cyrus at his desk, scribbling away on some paper. Everything seems as normal as it was before. He shakes his head to reorient himself, takes a deep breath, and removes his earpiece.

A notification then dings on the tablet that is lying on his desk.

INITIATION COMPLETE. WELCOME TO LEADERSHIP.

Unbeknownst to James, his earpiece had injected a serum into his brain. The serum traveled directly into James's frontal cortex rendering him unconscious but still mentally active. It allowed James's subconscious mind to be transported into a virtual world that is constructed, controlled, and interacted with by top leadership members. They could not only witness this ceremony but could also willingly participate as they please.

James is now officially an initiated member of Leadership.

***

James arrives home and meets Sybil in their bedroom. She is sitting on the bed and staring out the window in deep thought. He immediately feels guilty.

"Should we go for a stroll, darling?" he asks. "Weather's nice."

Sybil rolls her eyes before turning around. "Right," she says. "I'll get my coat."

James locks the door of their home as the two of them start for the street. As they venture down the sidewalk, James reaches down for Sybil's hand, but she pulls away.

"Sybil. Darling. Look. I know these last few weeks have been rough. Quite rough," he says. "I never meant to… I was really just trying… ugh. I'm sorry. I'm truly sorry," he says at the end of his breath.

"What are you sorry for?" she asks, still looking away.

"You know what I'm sorry for," he says.

She raises her eyebrows.

"I should never have hit you. That- that was too far."

"Yes," she says.

"Yes? So, we're good?"

"I need to think," she says, looking at the trees and foliage that line the street. A gust of wind blows that makes Sybil cling to her coat. Her nose turns red and her cheeks flare.

At that moment, an old, ripped, raggedy green ball rolls into James's feet. He looks up to see five children staring back at him from a small field.

43

"Throw it here!" one that looks to be about eight shouts from the grass.

James smirks. He places his foot on top of the ball and boots it over the young child's head and onto the field.

"Go get it, boys!" James shouts, cupping his mouth.

The children run and chase after the ball, laughing and smiling. James looks over at Sybil, who cracks a soft smile.

"Shall we play a game of footie?" he jokes.

"You'd enjoy that, wouldn't you?" she teases as she grabs his arm and laughs.

"Every minute," he replies as they walk past the young boys and the soccer field and into the evening

5 SECRETS

James breaks for lunch and walks the halls with his workplace buddy, Eric Donner. Eric is a senior workplace official and was introduced to James through Lester Prime as someone to help James get acquainted with his new role. Eric has been a part of senior leadership at the workplace for around ten years and is well accustomed to the ever-changing atmosphere. He's a by-the-book kind of man, just over fifty years old with a wife twenty years his junior and a beard that seems to grow longer by the minute. His eyes are close together and are the darkest shade of green. He keeps himself tightly groomed and always carries a comb with him wherever he goes. Eric is quiet in general, mostly keeping to himself. But he has a dark sense of humor and is known to possess many secrets.

"Ah, the sweet smell of potatoes," Eric muses aloud as they approach the cafeteria. "I love potato Wednesdays."

"Isn't there potatoes every day?" asks James. "I hardly remember there being a day without them."

"Ah, who gives a fuck? How are you handling your newfound fame, superstar?"

"Fame? I'd hardly call it fame," James says as he glances over at a poster depicting him standing on the weekend rally stage wielding the bloody sword he had used to strike down Charlie.

His stomach drops as he pictures Charlie's head falling to the floor. He feels a sharp cramp in his gut and grimaces.

Eric and James approach the cafeteria counter and scan their PC cards. They receive their extra rations of food due to their status of Leadership and make their way to the private Leadership eating room. It is situated directly next to the one used by general public workers.

The refectory is painted army green with numerous plaques and military décor that flood the open spaces on the walls. An extremely large television that takes up half of the room is turned on. It is playing footage of high-ranking Regiment members boarding planes that are bound for other countries. James listens in.

"Senior official Martin Melnick is boarding the new Regiment spider jet today, headed for the Japanese province of China. Mr. Melnick is bravely representing our great nation today as we continue to engage in trade talks with the foreign Chinese trade giant."

James has never heard these kinds of political conversations as a civilian. After all, foreign affairs are never mentioned in the Regiment-issued newspaper, and James is entirely uneducated on most of the countries that presently exist in the world today. He realizes that this is all new to him as he sharpens his focus on the television.

"Yeah, turns out we're not the only country in the world," Eric says as he notices James taking an interest in what's on the television screen.

"I can't believe I never had any interest in finding out more about the world," says James as he bites into his food. "I guess I've really only cared about New Haven, but this… this is so interesting now."

"Yes friend, it's a big wide world out there," Eric states. "Try not to crap your pants, but aliens are real."

James turns sharply from the television. "What?" he asks. "What do you mean aliens are real?"

"Oh yeah, they're real alright. That's what you felt tickling your ass last night. See they call that a probing," Eric says, making air quotes while trying not to laugh.

James makes a face at Eric as he picks up a piece of potato and throws it at him.

"So, what's the deal with this Melnick guy? He's got to be senior Leadership, right?"

Eric continues to chew his food and stare at the screen. Chatter surrounds them as other members of Leadership are sitting down to enjoy their lunches.

"I mean how else do you get to board a plane and leave the country?" James asks.

"Correct," Eric says. "Melnick is pretty badass. I trained with him a few years ago actually. Guy is sharp as a tack. He's an architect by trade; he actually designed a good portion of The Palace!"

"Oh really?" James asks, very interested. "So, who sent him to China? Like, who is his boss?"

"Can't say. But whoever it is, is a very, very powerful man," Eric replies. "Or woman," he adds with a wink.

James thinks for a moment and then leans forward in his chair to get closer to Eric.

"There must be a huge hierarchical structure to this thing, right?" James blurts out. "I wonder who is at the top. I wonder what our plans are with China. Do we have any natural allies?"

"Woah, woah, woah, man keep your voice down," says Eric, looking around.

James retracts and stiffens his shoulders.

"You joined Leadership ten seconds ago, you don't want to be asking all these questions so soon. Don't worry friend, I'll show your eyes what they need to see, for now."

James looks down at his plate of food.

"You know what? Meet me at the Good Park after work today. But don't tell anyone where you are going and make sure you're not followed. It's my job to show you the ropes after all.

"Yes! Ok good, I'll be there," says James with widened eyes and a giddy tone. "You can have the rest of my potatoes; I'm headed back to work." James gives his tray to Eric and pushes back his chair.

"Happy potato Wednesday friend," James says to Eric as he leaves the eating room and starts for the slide.

James goes through the rest of the day with wonder at the front of his mind. He can hardly focus on his tasks during the day due to the anticipation of meeting Eric at the Good Park. He wonders what secrets he will learn. Is today the day he will uncover how the entire operation works? Who is truly in charge? What motivations burn the brightest?

***

James slips on his coat and exits through the front door. He makes his way down the street, dusted with light snow. Trees, draped in white, flank the thoroughfare. James picks up the pace, counting one foot in front of the other as the Good Park finally comes into view. Black pointed gates surround the property, giving it a haunting appearance.

James enters the park and follows the sidewalk through bunches of hedges and open fields to an empty bench. He sits down on one side of the bench, places his briefcase next to him, and waits in silence. The sounds of sprinkling snow and lightly blowing winds hypnotize him. The temperature seems to drop as James moves his hands to the inside of his coat jacket. A figure appears at the other side of the empty park. Eric is coming to meet him. James's heart begins to race.

"Hello, my friend," says Eric as he occupies space on the bench.

"Long time no see," says James. "It's getting quite cold out, eh?" he says, sniffling.

"Ah yes, the winds of change," Eric responds, adjusting himself in his seat. "You think you're ready to know what you signed up for?"

"Yes. My ears are open, my mouth is shut, and my mind is ready," replies James.

Eric swivels his head as though to ascertain their solitude. Seemingly satisfied, he sits forward, looking at his gloved hands before he speaks.

"What I am about to show you cannot leave this conversation. That means you can't tell Sybil what you see here. You can't tell your mother, hell, I don't even want you to tell yourself in the mirror when you're lonely." Eric makes direct eye contact with James.

"You have my word."

Eric clears his throat and adjusts his position on the bench. He reaches into his pocket and pulls out an earpiece. "Put this in your left ear and start breathing deeply."

James does as he is instructed. He takes the earpiece, swallows some air, and places the earpiece in his left ear before sitting back on the bench, awaiting what is to come. He closes his eyes.

James finds himself alone in a dark room. He can't see anything but a few inches in front of his eyes. He squints, and suddenly there is Eric, right by his side. Eric grunts as he composes himself and then claps twice, forcing the brightest of lights to appear, temporarily blinding James's unsuspecting eyes.

"Ah sorry about that, should've warned you," says Eric as he opens his eyes.

James opens his eyes slowly and takes in the surrounding environment. They are standing on what looks and feels like a cloud and staring at five large screens. Everything has a pearly sheen, blinding white as if they were lounging in heaven. The screens have floating labels underneath them and read:

The history of New Haven

The Grand Endeavor

Our enemies

Our friends

Solution

"Choose one," Eric says with hubris as he stands behind James. "Choose one to explore today, and we will complete the others at some other time."

James's eyes light up like a kid at a candy store. He steps forward to examine the screens. As he gets closer, he finds himself restricted by an invisible barrier. He stands there for a brief moment as he thinks about which screen could possibly provide the most interesting information.

History of New Haven sounds fun. I wonder if they included the part where they tear innocent people from their homes and force them into labor.

"Hmm," he says, still deep in thought.

Our enemies ha. Who isn't an enemy?

Our friends. Yeah right.

Solution? That sounds kinda fucked up.

James places his hands on his hips. "I'll take screen two," he says confidently.

"Alright then. Once I take you, we cannot go back. Are you sure?" asks Eric.

"Screen two," James says crossing his arms.

Eric places his hat on his head, approaches screen two, and motions for James to join him. The invisible barrier is gone as James and Eric stand before the screen. Eric places his hand on screen two and instructs James to do the same.

A flash and they are transported into the screen and dragged to the other side.

James and Eric float above a large boardroom and look down at eight people seated around a perfectly finished brown oak wooden desk. The room is dimly lit as the shadows of figures dance on the walls. It is clear they are observing some sort of meeting but are not detected by the people in the room. It is like being an invisible fly on a wall.

"What you are seeing now is the first grand meeting of Leadership that took place nearly forty years ago back in 2056. See that elderly looking man seated there at the head of the table?"

James nods.

"That's Warren, Wizard, Grey. The father of New Haven. To his right is the first elder Alexander Scheible. Then second elder Laurel Scheible next to him. They're brother and sister. And look next to her. That's Paige Wellersby, an officer of the truth. She's distantly related to the Scheible twins somehow. And over there, on the other side of the table, that ginger-looking fellow drinking the ale. That's Torus Gline. He is the head of state affairs."

James strokes his chin as Eric continues speaking.

"Then his wife, Tina Gline seated next to him. She was the one to find the scroll of the great prophecy. They are followed by their son Horus, the town nitwit. Finally, on the other head of the table, is the Wizard's wife, Bolin Grey. She's the most dangerous woman on the planet."

Eric turns his gaze from the table and looks directly at James. "This is where The Grand Endeavor was born.

James squints his eyes and brushes his hair back from his face as he listens in to the conversation happening below.

"I have heard what you speak, good counsel," says Wizard Grey. "The time for judgment is upon us."

Wizard places his hand on a large book that lies beside him on the table. "If not for Tina, hearing the great words of the prophecy, we would not be here today ready to make the necessary changes that lie before us," he says, waving the book at the table. "It is, after all, up to us, to change the world."

"Here, here!" says Alexander as he lifts his glass. "To Tina!"

Those at the table toast and sip from their individual glasses. Torus drains his goblet and begins pouring himself another glass.

Wizard stands from his seat and moves his eyes to every person in the room, soaking in a few seconds of silence. His fists are clenched and are resting on the table in front of him. "The grand god is pleased with our work, my friends, very pleased indeed. He has told me so. In a dream. In this dream, I ventured into the flames of battle and saw the images of a great victory. I have seen through the flames, visions of the good new way. I have seen visions of you all, mounted on piles of gold. We do this to please the grand god. In his name we pray."

Everyone in the room stands together and tightly clasps their hands as they bow their heads in unison. The door opens, and two men appear, dragging an unconscious body toward the table. They pick up the body and place it on the table so that the head lies in front of Wizard and the feet lie in front of Bolin. The two men bow and then quickly leave the room. The eight members of the table lift their heads and open their eyes simultaneously, staring at the body before them.

Wizard picks up a large blade from the table and holds it firmly in his right hand.

"A sacrifice for the grand god," he states, as he places his knife hand on the chest of the unknown body. He feels the heart beating through the skin, vibrating on the heel of his hand that lays still on the chest. He turns his hand so that the tip of the knife is now directly over the heart. He applies slow and direct pressure with the blade and enters the chest cavity of the hostage. He goes around the sternum with intentional slices of the blade to carve out the heart.

James watches in horror as he feels his blood boiling from within. He does not expect to see something as gruesome as this and works hard to hide his emotions as they begin to show in his face. Eric looks over at James, studying his reaction before turning his attention back to the table.

Wizard carves a large circle into the chest of the body on the table. The man is now squirming with pain but still under strong sedative control. Wizard places the bloody knife down on the table before reaching inside the chest cavity with his hands. He grasps the unknown man's heart that is beating ferociously in his chest. Wizard clasps down with his fingers and rips the vital organ out of his chest, detaching it from arteries and veins, before holding it straight in the air.

The cells of the heart muscle are still contracting and pumping blood even with it now being unbound to a body. Wizard holds the heart close to his face.

"We will now please the grand god and drink the blood of every apostate until they cease to exist!" he exclaims to the room. "We are building a new bright future together my friends. One where the grand god is worshiped by those who deserve his light. One where his way is the way of all things. One where he chooses his disciples and the grand god's choices are never false. He has chosen us, and we will not fail him."

Another flash, and James and Eric are transported back to the Good Park.

They each remove their earpieces and adjust to their new environment. Their skin stings from the coldness of the weather.

"I have so many questions," James says, nearly out of breath.

"I can say I definitely expected that," replies Eric. "What you just witnessed there is called a ceremony. I know--what a clever name. You know they really should consult more people before they name anything else."

James laughs to himself and looks out at the falling snow.

"So, friend, there's a bit of a religious component to this. I think you're ready to hear it because soon, you'll be expected to practice what we teach you," says Eric.

James says nothing but manages a nod as he waits for Eric to say more.

"You see, we have been chosen for a great mission James. We have been chosen to lead a world of people in the service of the grand god. The grand god speaks to us. We listen and obey. You have been chosen to join what we call The Grand Endeavor which is how we serve him," says Eric as he points up to the sky. "We serve him as his chosen disciples, and we do so nobly. We are not promised anything in the afterlife or anything like that, but it is said that his chosen few are rewarded handsomely."

James takes a few beats to digest what Eric just divulged.

"…The grand god, you say. So why do only the chosen disciples worship him? Wouldn't we want all the people of New Haven to know about the grand god? Why is it a secret?"

"We are but humans," Eric says. "Tiny ants on a great big field. We have rules, we have families, we have love and all that, but at the end of the day, we're just apes on a floating rock. The Grand God is a God for god's sake! The master, the creator of all things! Who are we to question his judgement?"

"The Grand God chooses who he sees as most fit to carry out his cause. Would you trust this great cause to just anyone? Would you give this great responsibility to the woman cleaning your toilet? No! We are lucky, James. Lucky! You will see this in time. I promise you that," says Eric, as he sits back in his seat.

James senses the shifting of energies and decides to leave the rest of his questions for later. It is clear that Eric is devoted to this "Grand Endeavor" and expects James to follow suit.

"Right, right. That makes perfect sense," James says. "I am honored to have been chosen. I shall try to serve in the best way that I can. Thank you for showing me all this."

Eric crinkles his nose hardens his face. He rises from the bench and places his hands in his pockets. "We will visit the other screens at some other time. I'm sure you'll have questions about those too. For now, my nuts are freezing, and I've got to get going. I'll leave you with this," he says brushing the snow from his coat. "Every opportunity that comes your way from here on out, it's probably best that you take them. You may not understand why you are being asked to do certain things and you may have questions too. That's quite alright. But James," says Eric standing directly over him. "Direct your questions to me. No one else. You hear? Not everyone is as friendly as I've been. The Great God chooses correctly but he can un-choose."

James looks back at him and nods.

"Go with Grace," says Eric as he reaches out his hand, motioning James to repeat the phrase.

"Go with Grace," he replies as the side of his mouth twitches into a smile.

Eric retreats and they both go their separate ways. James places his hands in his pockets and is surprised to feel the earpiece touch his finger. He realizes that he has not given it back to Eric and promptly turns around to find him.

Eric is gone. Swallowed by a flurry of snow.

6 THE FUND

On a blustery morning, Sybil arrives at her place of employment—the Fund, where she works as a Tell-girl. The ostentatious edifice displays its prestige outside and in. Glorious lighting displays, and perfectly crafted New Haven flags surround the building.

There are plenty of landmarks and constructions in New Haven that give off this appearance of prestige and vast wealth. That is something the early leaders prioritized. They always say: A wealthy nation is a healthy nation. So long as it looks like it. New Haven looks like it.

In reality, New Haven is rotting. Postponed construction projects, very little upkeep of buildings and inefficient guidelines make it hard to keep track of anything that might need a boost. But as long as it looks right from the outside, nobody seems to care. Appearance is everything after all.

Every morning Sybil ventures up two sets of extraordinarily wide stairs that span thirty-five feet across and sport twenty steps on each. A bronze handrail stands directly in the center of each pair of stairs and is molded to fit any shape of hand comfortably. Sybil likens this experience as her morning workout and loves to count each step as she goes.

She finally arrives at the enormous twelve-foot-tall front doors of the Fund. They are made of pure gold and have immaculate silver handles. Two guards stand in flawlessly creased uniforms at each side of the doorway.

"Good morning Mrs. Cleary," one of the guards says as the other holds open the door. "It's a good day to be great!" he says with a smile as he guides her inside.

"Good morning gentlemen," Sybil responds as she enters the building.

Sybil turns to her right and approaches the coat hanging station. She scans her PC on the card reader and places her coat on a smart-hanger that dangles up ahead of her. She pushes the stow button on the machine and the hanger retreats on a rail to safekeep her coat for later.

A soft child-like voice comes from behind Sybil.

"Good morning Mrs. Cleary. I have three messages for you and have set up your station."

Sybil doesn't turn around to greet the voice. "That's great Missy," Sybil says as she grabs her bag. "I'll have my Green Grass now. Thanks."

Missy is Sybil's assistant at The Fund. She answers Sybil's phone, sets up Sybil's desk, files Sybil's paperwork and most importantly, retrieves Sybil's beverages. She is 20 years old, and her strawberry blonde hair flows like the wind from her head. Her tall and physically fit physique makes her ideal for a place like The Palace. But she needs to earn her way to a profession like that. Missy, fresh out of school, was assigned 6 months ago to start her internship at The Fund as Sybil's assistant. She is being closely evaluated and watched by senior Regiment members. Admittingly mostly by males. This is not something new for Missy.

As a child, she was placed in Pathways for Life after her parents were sent to labor camps by The Regiment. Pathways for Life is a school that all children must attend as it determines what jobs they eventually will undertake in the future. It is rigorous and strict. Excessively long and supposedly standardized examinations rule the days. Personality assessments and mindless unguided lectures rule the nights. It was here where Missy foolishly attempted to search for the sounds of music that had once captured her spirit.

When Missy was very young, her mother played music for her in secret on a tablet device called an iBeat. It was made of glass but foldable in any direction. A unique device from the old world. It famously contained the largest musical library ever created without downloads or physical copies necessary. There was a time where an iBeat was in the home of every single American. But now, they're impossible to find as music is considered mind poison and is strictly outlawed in New Haven. She can't remember what song it was that she heard for the first time, but she recalls exactly how it made her feel. She remembers the rhythm and melodies that captivated her mind. Even at such a low volume. She remembers feeling the need to move her body in ways that are now deemed unnatural. She remembers her foot tapping along with the beat of the song and the smile that would beam from her mother. It is so wide and bright. It's as if she's capable of emitting the warmth of the sun. She is captivated instantly. After her parents were taken from her, Missy never heard the sounds of music again.

One day in school, Missy drew up enough courage to ask her instructor, Leadership member Trough, about music. Her curiosity led her to inquire as to why it is outlawed and if he has ever experienced music himself. Her face was then promptly met with the blunt end of a ruler. As she fell down and held her face, screaming in pain, he leaned down to her level and spoke softly. "With your chubby body and foolish temperament, you would be a great fit for The Fund."

This mantra was repeated to her daily for years.

Chubby body. Foolish temperament.

Chubby body. Foolish temperament.

Chubby body. Foolish temperament.

She could change her body as that was in her control. But The Fund, she would learn to accept, is her fate.

"Missy, my Green Grass!" Sybil barks from her desk, snapping her fingers as she reviews some documents.

Sybil is studying a Desk Report which essentially is a small report that is put on every Tell-girl's desk by Leadership, detailing the amount of New Haven Bills or NHB's that are distributed into the hands of citizens on any given day. Leadership always maintains that the value of NHBs is worth a bit less in purchasing power as a physical bill, than if it were on a PC electronically. They manage this by imposing a small tax on any purchases made with NHBs. This is especially important information because Leadership members know how valuable NHBs are outside of New Haven. Most of the other countries in the world are experiencing lacking economies and New Haven prides itself on being a modern economic superpower with its export of Working Women to neighboring countries.

Missy arrives at Sybil's desk with a cup of Green Grass in hand. "Here you are Mrs. Cleary. Just how you like it."

Sybil does not break her gaze with her desk report as she grabs the cup and takes a sip of her morning beverage. She lets out a large exhale after the first sip.

"Thank you, Missy. Go prepare the Tell-Station now please."

Missy exits Sybil's tight office space and ventures to the main lobby area where all the Tell-Girls have their stations. She approaches Tell-Station number seven and opens the door. She starts to quietly hum a familiar melody. Missy notices the paint from inside the rectangular shaped box is tearing at the edges and that the wood used to construct the apparatus is rotting with mold. This can only be seen from inside the station however as the outside is pristine and practically sparkling.

Missy is finishing preparing Sybil's Tell-Station when an elderly man appears at the window. He is sharply dressed, wearing a black overcoat and slacks. His head is bald on top, but he has patches of hair on the sides that are as white as the snow that's falling outside. He grips a maroon-colored cane with his right hand that he uses to support his weight as his other hand rests comfortably in his pocket. His age has deformed his spine as he bends slightly over his cane.

"Hello there," he says through the window. His grumbly voice, muffled from the dividing glass window. "I am here to make a withdrawal."

"Great, just a moment sir. I'll go and fetch Mrs. Cleary."

Missy scoots back to Sybil's office. "Your 8:30 appointment is here Mrs. Cleary. He is going to be making a withdrawal today."

"Right," replies Sybil. "Right, thank you," she says as she takes down the last few sips of her drink.

Sybil makes her way to the tell-station and puts on her tell-hat. She enters the booth and hears the screeching sound of the front window as she opens it for business.

"Ah, yes, good morning, Mr. Crane. It's wonderful to see you," says Sybil, as she starts coughing continuously through her breath.

"Bloody hell, have you caught a cold?" replies the old man.

"No, no," she says wiping her mouth and regaining her composure. "I swallowed some spit is all. What can I do for you today Mr. Crane?"

"Ah, yes. Well Mrs. Cleary, today I'd like to make a rather large withdrawal. How much do I have on this here card?" he asks as he hands Sybil his PC with his shaky and elderly hand.

Sybil scans the PC on the reader bringing up Mr. Crane's financial information on her screen.

"Ok, erm, I'm required to inform you that a withdrawal of NHBs does limit your purchasing power. The value of our currency does more for you when on a PC instead of in cash form. Do you understand what I have informed you?"

"Yes, ma'am I do," says the old man with a smile.

Sybil clacks away on her keyboard.

"Your total balance sir is $227,394."

"Alright," says Mr. Crane, "I'll take it all."

"You'll take it all?" Sybil asks politely. "You know you can't withdrawal all of your funds, right Mr. Crane?"

"Well, why the hell not?" He snaps.

"Mr. Crane, I'm pretty sure we've been over this before," she says smiling as she tries to lighten the situation.

His face doesn't change from a frown.

"You see, if you have no balance on your PC, then you'll have no funds to support your bills or obligations. How will your rent be paid? What about your food? If The Regiment were to let you take out all your money at once, how could you be trusted to be able to afford whatever lifestyle you would choose to lead? Look at the plebs for example Mr. Crane. They have no PCs, so they live in squalor. They choose their lifestyles every day and look at where they live. Some of them cannot even afford food."

"I don't care about any of that!" says Mr. Crane. "It's my money, I'd like to have it now please," he says raising his voice.

Sybil remains silent. It is clear that this is going to be an issue as more eyes turn toward Sybil's booth.

"Mr. Crane, kindly lower your voice," says Sybil. "You know that I don't make the rules. You know that one of the benefits of living in New Haven is that your finances are taken care of."

Sybil leans in close to the old man so that only he can hear her. "Are you trying to throw that all away?"

The old man leans in to meet Sybil. His neck bends over even further than before. "Get me my fucking money, now." He taps his cane on the window.

Sybil retreats to her original posture and draws a deep breath. "Don't make me do this Mr. Crane. Please, you must know what can happen. I can give you 50% of your holdings in NHBs since your balance is over $200,000 but nothing more."

"I'm not leaving here without my money."

"You know you can't leave New Haven," she whispers. "What do you need all of this cash for anyways?"

The old man takes a deep breath and looks around the room. His tired eyes finally come back around to meet Sybil's.

"GIVE ME MY FUCKING MONEY!" He screams, slamming his fist on the table and dropping his cane to the floor.

Just then, everyone on the first floor of The Fund turns to stare at Mr. Crane and Sybil. Within a second or two, three large men in full Regiment uniforms appear from behind Sybil's station and proceed to jog over to Mr. Crane.

"What's going on here?" one demands.

"No, no it's quite alright. Mr. Crane here is just a little upset," says Sybil. "I'm sure he'll be calm now, right Mr. Crane?" she asks at the old man, her eyes wide and piercing as if to tell the old man to think carefully about his next move.

"I've had it with you all! I'm here to take what's rightfully mine. Load up my cash this instant!"

Sybil drops her head in defeat as she has seen this kind of outburst before. She knows it will not end well for Mr. Crane.

At that moment, one of the Regiment members grabs Mr. Crane's hands and forces them into the air. Without saying another word, the other two Regiment members each grab a leg as they carry the kicking and screaming Mr. Crane into a room toward the back of the lobby titled "Propadat' room

1".

Sybil will never see Mr. Crane again.

She composes herself and moves her hair out of her face as a message appears on her tell-screen computer monitor. It reads:

HANDLE YOURSELF BETER AND REACT QUICKER NEXT TIME SYBIL. WE DON'T WANT ANY MORE MISTAKES. – LEADERSHIP

Sybil frowns and lightly smacks her forehead with her palm.

They can't even spell correctly.

7 RELIEF

Sybil retrieves her coat and exits the doors of The Fund. She looks out at the bronze handrails and golden steps before her.

They don't look as shiny from this side.

She makes her way down the steps and turns the corner gliding close to the side of the building. She moves east on Bleak Street and makes her way toward Gline Avenue. An uncomfortable feeling slowly crawls into the depths of her mind. She walks ten paces, stops, and turns around.

Is someone watching me?

It's thirty-five degrees Fahrenheit outside, but the wind chill makes it feel closer to twenty. She places her hands in her pocket for warmth as she scans her surrounding area. Sybil notices the trails of rockets in the distant sky. She sees a few work colleagues entering their respective shuttles and vehicles as they head for home. She feels the sense of abandonment as the streets quickly become barren. The trees look lonely and cold, and a piece of paper floats by her as it's carried by swift gusts of wind. She is alone.

Sybil turns back around and continues walking in the direction of her home. The sky is nearly black now and the streetlights are dim. The asphalt of the street crumbles beneath her shoes with each step that she takes forward. Sybil continues on as chills race down her spine.

It's not too much further.

She picks up her pace. Her feet become lighter.

Left foot, right foot, left foot, right foot.

She counts her steps. Faster now.

Left foot, right foot, left foot, right foot.

Her breathing is shallow as it becomes more and more labored.

Left foot, right foot, left foot, right foot.

She passes an abandoned postal building. Her shadow chases her up the solid brick walls of the building. Higher and higher.

Left foot, right foot.

Her heart begins to race, and it feels like it might burst from the tight confines of her chest.

Left foot, right foot.

She enters an alley now, 50 yards away from an opening where she will find herself closer to her home street. Her steps echo off the brick and wet pavement below her.

Left foot, right foot, left foot, right-

"Hey." whispers a voice. The sound is sharp and bounces off the walls of the alley stinging her ears.

Sybil yelps and stops in her tracks. "Who's there?"

She spins around. "Come on! Who's there?"

A shadow emerges from behind her. Stepping toward her.

Sybil withdraws. "I know you're there! Please don't hurt me, I have nothing for you."

The figure moves closer. Quiet but quick.

Sybil continues backtracking. Her heartbeat is now ferociously thumping and near the top of her throat. She curls her hands into fists and prepares herself for imminent contact. The figure is directly behind Sybil now.

Just then, two hands come across Sybil's face and clasp over her mouth.

Sybil swings her arms as she feels the overpowering strength of a man dominate her, forcing her to her knees. She whips and whirls.

"Shhhh. Sybil. Don't be afraid. It's me," whispers a voice.

Sybil is still ferociously squirming, trying to break the man's strong and firm hold.

"Sybil, my love. Stop! It's me!"

Sybil suddenly recognizes the voice.

"C- Cam? Is that you?"

The hold becomes lighter.

"I'm going to release you now, please, don't scream."

Cam releases his grasp on Sybil and steps backwards, giving her some space to breathe. His arms are tired from holding her down. They look at one another for a moment, neither of them speaking a word. After a pause, Sybil rises to her feet and inches closer to Cam, all the while maintaining eye contact as they study each other's faces. They are actually seeing each other for the first time in reality. No headset, no virtual environment, this is finally real life.

Sybil reaches for Cam's face and rests her hand on his cheek. He looks exactly the same in person as he does virtually. His perfect bone structure. His light brown hair. His wide and inviting eyes. His deep and intense stare.

"It's really you," she says as she runs her fingers along the contours of his jaw.

"It's really me," he says, placing his hand on top of hers. She can feel the warmth from his hand ooze into her own skin.

Her stomach turns inside out as her skin blushes through the splintering of the cold. She runs her hands south to the collar of his shirt as the blended smells of mahogany and teakwood invade her senses.

"How- how did you find me?" Sybil asks as she caresses the back of Cam's neck. His muscular build acting as speed bumps to her touch.

"I had to," he replies, cracking a smile. Cam moves his grip around Sybil's waist. Their eyes are locked now, as they begin to breathe in sync. The cold forces them closer and closer together until they meet in a tight embrace. The two of them entirely unaware and unconcerned with the surrounding environment.

Sybil removes her head from Cam's shoulder and looks up at him. He stares back down at her while still gripping her waist with his strong and muscular hands. He pulls her closer to him. They want each other badly. Here and now.

"I- I don't know what to say," Sybil whispers.

"Then don't," he says as he leans into Sybil's lips. They fall to the floor and their shadows disappear

8 SCREEN FIVE

James sits at his desk, biting away at his nails as he shifts tabs on his computer screen. The rest of the office shuffles out for the night.

Finally, alone.

He drops his head atop his hands as stress and fatigue overtake him. He can't stop thinking about the earpiece he took from the park. Does Eric know this whole time? Is he secretly giving the earpiece to James so that he can explore the other four screens?

James sits back in his chair and exhales. His hand then drifts below the desk to the top drawer. He stops himself for a moment, gripping the handle, before deciding to open it. A small black bag carrying the earpiece lies there starkly in his view. It's so light in weight but it carries the heaviest of implications, all of which flood his mind.

His curiosity overtakes him as he places the earpiece in his left ear and accepts whatever is to come.

Two claps of the hand and James finds himself in the blindingly white virtual world again but this time, without Eric. The five screens are there in front of him, just like before. Only this time, screen 2 is no longer bolded.

The history of New Haven

The Grand Endeavor

Our enemies

Our friends

Solution

James wonders if the screens will even work without Eric present.

Eric had to enter the screen first last time, right?

James looks around. Blindingly white. Solitude.

He inches closer toward the screens.

James takes a few seconds to think before starting to advance toward screen 5 which reads: Solution. As he approaches the screen, he can hear a buzz growing louder. He pauses for a moment, giving himself one last chance to turn around and go back to his desk.

"Fuck it."

Everything in James's environment is pitch black as he tumbles over himself in a seemingly gravity-free environment. James's eyes are closed as he tries to breathe but there is no oxygen. He is underwater. He begins to panic as droves of salty ocean water fill his lungs. His body tosses into barrel rolls as the waves of the ocean pound over him.

Then, everything goes black.

James awakes to brutal fits of coughing as seawater is violently expelled from his stomach and his lungs beg for air. His consciousness wavers in and out, but he can sense that he is being dragged.

Is this still the ocean?

Strong hands grip each of his arms. He hasn't the strength to resist.

"Wait! What's going on? Where are you taking me?"

"To meet your maker," says a voice.

James can hardly see through the blindfold that is tied around his head. But if he squints, he can faintly make out the scene of a beach at twilight as his knees scrape across the sand and onto the pavement.

The two men drag James to a nearby building and sit him down in an old wooden chair. The blindfold is removed and there in front of him sits Wizard. The same man he had seen from his time in screen 2, only this time he is seated in a golden throne, lifted eight feet off the ground making it hard to see him completely.

Wizard's throne is immaculate and has steps made of bones and cartilage plastered together that lead from his seat to the ground. He is surrounded by bodyguards and Leadership members all dressed in gold-plated armor and standing at attention.

"Hello James," says Wizard. "I was wondering when I'd get the chance to meet you."

"You know who I am?" asks James as he coughs out the last of the seawater and spits sprinkles of sand from his mouth.

"Of course, I do James. You're our exciting new recruit! Oh. I'm sorry about the- dragging you through the sand bit. I didn't exactly design that part of the experience," says Wizard, laughing to himself and looking around the room for approval. Scattered laughs come from the corners of the room.

"Experience? What do you mean experience?" James putters.

"You put in an earpiece in your ear to see me, did you not?" Wizard asks.

"Yes sir. I- uh. Yes, I believe I did," replies James sheepishly as he brushes the sand and water from his hair.

"Bingo! You see, unfortunately my physical body died during the revolution. It was old and raggedy anyway. Messy conquest," he says clearing his throat. "But alas! I did triumph after all! Here I stand before you, completely and utterly immortal!"

James deflates into his seat. It is clear Wizard is looking for James to be impressed with him, but he is so disoriented from inhaling seawater that all he can offer is bewilderment.

"How- how is that possible?" he says, wiping his mouth and coughing.

Wizard's hands fall from above his head into a heap on his lap. His excited expression morphs into a scowl.

"Many years ago, I hired a virtual design team to create everything that you currently see around you. This is my... dojo, of sorts. That earpiece that you placed in your ear to get here. It injected you with a special serum rendering your body unconscious, but it set your mind on fire!"

James tilts his head. His mouth is slightly ajar.

Wizard continues. "It connected your mind to a frequency that this particular program is running on. I have made myself permanently tethered here and can entertain guests as they come and go. I've evolved my being into the ultimate immortal digitalized preacher of our mission and the Grand God's will for our Grand Endeavor. I'm here to teach you the Solution."

James is fully awake now, realizing that he is conversing with the founder of The Regiment. The man behind Leadership and his way of life as he currently knows it. He understands that he is speaking with the most influential man this world has ever seen.

"Well, I'm pleased to meet you then. You've created quite a- thing," he says as he looks around. "So, this is where you live then?"

"Now he's catching on!" says Wizard boisterously to the rest of the room filled with guards and Leadership members.

"And you James. You live on Gline Avenue, and you never fuck your wife," says Wizard changing his tone and hardening his face. "Tell me son, why is this what you have chosen for yourself?"

"I… I do my wife plenty," says James holding his hand over his chest.

Wizard sits back in his chair and smirks at James like he has a deck of aces up his sleeve.

"James, allow me to enlighten you."

Wizard takes a gulp of air.

"There is a camera in every room of every house in every faction of our good country. There is a web of smart applications reading every bit of that information and compiling it into reports. Those reports are then filed and sent over to an undisclosed secret destination every 2.683 seconds. That information is then filtered by my artificial intelligence program and downloaded to a very, very, VERY large computer. Mine," he says, showing his teeth.

"There are members of Leadership undercover as General Public workers in every department of every workplace. All of them report directly to me. I know everything."

They sit staring at each other in silence for a few seconds before Wizard continues his rant.

"This is the part where you see where you are James. This is the part where you realize that you have been chosen to be a part of a very special collective. This is when you decide- are you good, or are you... not good?"

"I am... good," replies James awkwardly. "Please, tell me the Solution that you've referenced. I'm interested to learn as much as I can about it."

"We will do that my child. We will. You have my word. I just need to have something of yours first," says Wizard ominously as he stands up straight from his throne and looks down at James. He appears stronger when standing. His elderly face is vibrant with energy. His long white cloak covers his feet completely and is held close to his body by a thick and brown feathered belt. He wears a perfectly white crown with 8 sharpened spikes that illuminate in the darkness. A single red jewel sticks to the front of the crown. It has an aura of its own.

"I need your loyalty. Pledge to me here and now, in front of the Grand God, that I am your eternal leader. Take this knife that I give you and let it pierce the skin of your palm. Draw enough blood to tinge my drink." He holds out his chalice. "Do this now, and I will open your eyes to the ways of the world."

James makes no movement, attempting to quickly digest all of this new information.

What the fuck is going on?

Am I going to die here?

Then, without further hesitation, he walks up the stairs made of bone and cartilage and kneels before Wizard's throne. His knee feels hard against the platform.

"I pledge my loyalty to you Wizard. I will service you and the Grand God in this endeavor. You have my undying support."

Wizard's smile grows wide as he hands James a beautiful and exquisite ten-inch blade. James takes the blade and makes a long cut across the palm of his left hand. Blood begins to drain profusely from the depth of the laceration. James holds his bleeding hand high as Wizard collects the fluid into his chalice.

"Good, my child. Sit," he commands as he motions James to return to his wooden chair. Wizard spins his chalice in a clockwise direction as if he has the finest glass of red wine in his possession. He inhales the aromas that escape from the chalice as he spins James's blood around and around. His toes curl with excitement. He puts the chalice to his lips and begins to drink, finishing every last drop.

James feels nauseous and turns his head away from Wizard as he carefully traverses the cartilage steps down toward his chair.

"Ahhh," says Wizard, as he places the cup back down. James applies pressure to his self-inflicted wound.

"My child," he says as he stands from his throne using only his cane to support himself. "The world is a funny place, and it has been for some time. Men and women alike walk around thinking they know what is best for them. Time and time again, they fall flat on their face.

James nods in agreement.

Before we started our good work with the Grand God, the divorce rate was 65%. That's almost seven marriages out of ten, boom, doomed for failure. Before our good work, domestic violence was at an all-time high, divorce lawyers were the most lucrative profession, and people in general just didn't get along. Did you know that 87% of workers in this country hated their jobs! Can you imagine James, a world where you go to work hating your job, then come home and hate your spouse? Imagine it! And the best part is, that's only half of the equation! This country's economy was turning to shit! All we did was print, print, print with zero innovation, no new ideas. No growth, no progress, no love, it's like we were living in hell on earth!"

James doesn't speak but continues nodding.

"So what's the solution? Well, the Grand God decides enough is enough and sends Tina- my granddaughter- a prophecy when she is but a baby. The date was October 25th, 2055. My 60th birthday. That morning, my daughter Laurel and her husband Thomas introduced me to my first granddaughter. They call her Tina. I was so excited to hold that child I could hardly breathe! When my daughter Laurel put Tina in my hands for the first time, I was overcome with so much emotion that I fell to floor, dropping us both." His face turns stiff. "The doctors said I had a grand mal seizure, and I can tell you I don't remember falling down," he says with a chuckle like an old man at a nursing home telling a joke.

"But it is then that I am taken under the wings of the Grand God," he says raising his voice with passionate intensity and raising his hands in the air.

"You see, when I touched Tina for the very first time, I was transported to another dimension. A dimension where the Grand God unveiled his plans for us to carry out in his name. All of that leads you and me to where we stand today. Isn't that glorious James?"

James scratches his neck. "What exactly does the prophecy say?

"Well James the specifics are only to be known by me - for now," Wizard says. "The Grand God speaks through me, and me alone. That is why he has made me immortal so that I can continue to give direction for New Haven and all its future glory. What you need to know now is that the Solution is to create a world where the Grand God has ultimate... ultimate..."

"Control?" James blurts without thinking. He grits his teeth and softens his eyes.

"Yes! Very good James. Ultimate control. That, is what the Grand God demands!

James lets out a relieved breath.

Wizard continues, "Look how happy everyone is now James. Look at the divorce rate, it's effectively nil. Zero. Look at how happy everyone is now that they know and trust, that WE know what is best for them. Happiness is, at the end of the day, what everyone strives for... right? That is what HE gives to us. Happiness. Therefore, we will work indefatigably to eliminate anyone that gets in the way of our happiness right James?" he asks. "There will always be naysayers, we just don't have to put up with them any longer."

Wizard stands, and he begins to walk down the steps and toward James until he is standing directly over him. "That is why you're here now my child." He puts his hand affectionately on James's shoulder. You are here now and being trusted by oh so many to fulfill your duty, in keeping New Haven... happy. Do you think you could do that son?"

James is uncomfortable with Wizard's hand on his shoulder. He wants to move away, but Wizard is staring at him so intensely that he feels intimidated by the power dynamic. James congeals.

"Of course, Wizard. Of course," says James. "I am here to help if I can. I would do anything to preserve the happiness of New Haven."

"Good, good," says Wizard as he removes his hand from James's shoulder and starts back up the stairs back to his throne. "At this weekend's rally, we are going to be sending a message to the General Public. The Grand God has called for a sacrifice and has named ten names. One of which is your wife. She will be sacrificed at this weekend's rally as a trai-"

"—Wait, who? Sybil?" James shoots back.

"DO NOT INTERRUPT ME BOY!" Wizard bellows at the top of his voice, slamming his cane on the ground, shaking James to his core and sending vibrations all over the room. James sits back in his seat as he realizes his emotional response caused him to overstep a boundary.

"I do not make these rules, I do not name these names! Are you questioning The Grand God's vision?" Wizard's face is burning with anger. His eyes practically pop from their place.

"No sir," James responds, retreating into his seat and staring straight into the floor.

"Sybil will be one of ten sacrifices for treason. The goal is to dissuade any further treasonous thoughts that may be floating amongst the general public from coming to fruition.

James still looks directly down at the floor. He holds his breath.

"Look James. You do not hold on to power by being everyone's friend. You see, in order for someone to ruin you, to stab you in the back, they must first be behind you. We stay ahead of our enemies. That is why we are ahead. That is why we are Leadership. And that, THAT is how we will dominate until the end of time!" Wizard wheezes.

The various guards in the room are fully stimulated from this passionate display of words and are all yelling "Huzzah" in symphony. The clamorous clanking of their armor strikes James's ears as they lift their fists to the ceiling.

"Now go!" exclaims Wizard to James, high on momentum. "Go and be a good husband to your wife, while you still can. You will receive an upgrade on Monday."

The two guards take James's arms again. They place the sandy blindfold back over his eyes and proceed to escort him out of the building and back to the beach. He tries to walk but their rapid pace is too hard to maintain without vision. His arms become bruised from the vicious clasps of fingers digging into his skin.

As James smells the freshness of the ocean air, the men release their grip.

"Remember, we are always watching," one cautions, as he pushes James toward the cold water of the ocean that is coming in from the rising tides on his bare feet. James suddenly feels a warm rushing sensation over his chest and next thing he knows, he is far, far away.

He opens his eyes to see the Woman sitting across from him.

Oh shit.

She is there, in his office the entire time. Waiting for him to return.

"I hope you've had a wonderful time," she says as she holds out her hand expecting James to return the earpiece.

James wipes his eyes, and takes the earpiece out of his ear, eagerly handing it over to The Woman. She places it in a small black bag and into her pocket.

"He thinks highly of you, you know. He thinks you could really be someone someday."

James opens his mouth to speak before she cuts him off.

"But for now," she says as she walks around James's desk facing him head-on. "You're mine."

She uses her hands to push James's knees together as she straddles him in his chair. Her weight is concentrated on his thighs as his feet go numb.

"Wait! Wait! Wait! What are you-"

"You have no say in this matter."

She proceeds to unzip James's trousers and remove her shirt, throwing it aggressively to the floor. She bites him on the right side of his neck as she proceeds to remove his pants.

James is panicking as he frantically looks around the room for someone to interrupt them. There's no one around. His breath becomes rapid to match the pace of his heart.

What can I do?

He realizes he is out of options and submits to her completely.

Cups and papers are cleared off of James's desk as he picks her up and places her on it. Every chair in the office turns on its head. Important documents parade in the air like confetti. Her on top of him. Him on top of her. The only time they are equal. The encounter covers every square inch of the office, all the while James can hardly tell if he is awake or asleep.

9 EXECUTION

James awakens on Saturday morning with a throbbing headache that makes him feel sick to his stomach. He sits up in bed and stares at the wall for a few seconds with Sybil still fast asleep at his side. She looks peaceful, dreaming about something that brings a smile to her face. He has never felt more guilt in his entire life than at that very moment.

Why did he fail to mention to her that she will be the star of today's weekend rally? Is it because he knows that there are cameras watching his every move hidden somewhere in his own house? Is it because he doesn't actually care for Sybil? Is his thirst for power and attention stronger than the love that he holds for her?

Even James isn't sure.

He looks around the room, trying to spot a camera, a hidden microphone or something out of the ordinary. There is nothing. James rubs his eyes and face vigorously with his hands and gets out of bed starting for the kitchen. He sits down at the breakfast table as his Green Grass is brewing on the counter. James glances out the window and notices a beautiful morning as the sun starts to rise. Everything is peaceful and quiet, which feels good for a moment, especially because there isn't a proxy in house barking orders. But James knows a horrible storm is on its way.

Just then, he feels a kiss land on the top of his head.

"Good morning, my love," says Sybil.

"Ah. Good morning love, you scared me."

Sybil flashes a cheeky smile. "Did you brew me a cup?"

"Yes, it's going now. Almost ready," he says smiling back, trying his best to act normal. James is a horrible actor.

"Is everything all right?"

"What do you mean?"

"You've been acting weird these last few days. How is everything going at work?"

"Oh- no darling, everything is fine. Work's great. I think I'm making a good impression. Let me see about that brew," he says standing up from his chair as it scratches across the wooden floor.

James takes a large pot of Green Grass out of the heating holster and proceeds to pour two cups. Sybil shrugs and opens the morning paper. She begins to read to herself.

"Looks like we have some executions again today," she says unenthusiastically. "God, I really wish all that would stop. I mean, if we keep executing people at this rate, there won't be anyone left to swing the axe."

James spits out his first sip of Green Grass all over himself.

"Ah- stupid, shi- fuck!" he exclaims, grabbing a towel to frantically clean his shirt.

James walks over with Sybil's Green Grass and places the cup down on the coaster in front of her.

"I'm going to get changed," he says. "We should be leaving soon. Drink up, love."

James returns to his bedroom and begins to get dressed for what he is sure to be a dreadful day. He opens one of the drawers and pulls out a freshly folded and neatly creased pair of slacks. As he starts to put them on, he looks out of his bedroom window. Horror covers his face as Leadership military vehicles and a shuttle are approaching his home. At the sight of this, he frantically rushes to the closet but only one of his legs is through his slacks. He trips over himself and smacks down hard on the floor. He quickly pushes himself up and fixes his pants before snatching a button-down shirt from the closet.

Sybil is still reading the paper and drinking her Green Grass when three loud knocks come at the front door.

"I'll get it!" James yells from the bedroom.

Sybil does not look up from her paper.

James arrives at the door and fixes the last of his buttons so he will appear somewhat presentable. He turns the handle and opens the door. There, stands Matthews and three other members of leadership. They are all armed with high powered rifles and seemingly ready for battle.

James is out of breath.

"Hello gentleman, can I help you?" he says wiping sweat from his upper lip.

"Is your wife home?" says Matthews faintly smiling.

"Yes. She's just there. At the table," he says as he opens the door to reveal Sybil in her seat.

She looks up. "Hello, gentleman!" she says with a wave.

Matthews stands in the doorway. "Great. We'll wait until you're both dressed and then we'll be escorting you to the rally today. VIP access. We'll see you both outside in fifteen minutes sharp," he says, retreating from the doorway.

James closes the door and flips the lock. He begins to hyperventilate as he hurries back to the bedroom without saying a word to Sybil.

Sybil furrows her brow and puts the paper back on the table. She swigs the last bit of her morning brew and goes to find James in the bedroom walk-in closet.

"What was that all about? We've never had an escort to the rally before," she says, as she takes off her robe and starts to get changed.

"Just get changed darling, we shouldn't be late," he replies sharply, trying his best not to look her in the eyes.

"James, look at me." demands Sybil as she plucks the tie out from his hand. "Tell me what is going on?"

James's eyes are bloodshot as he holds back the tears that are begging to be freed. They are alone in their closet. The two of them half dressed. Leadership members await them outside. Time seems to be moving rapidly, but James can take no more.

"Wait here," he says as he leaves her alone in the closet. He returns a few seconds later with a pencil and a scrap of newspaper that he had ripped off. He places the paper on the wall and begins writing feverishly as Sybil waits with endless anticipation.

He finishes writing and places the pencil on the top of his ear. "It's ok darling. I just had a bad dream last night about my parents and I miss them very, very much," he says as he hands her the piece of paper and widens his eyes.

Sybil takes the hint. "That's quite alright darling, I miss them, too," she says as she reads James's note. It reads:

You're going to be executed today for treason, but I am going to stop it. Act normal. They're watching!!

Sybil looks up from the paper horrified.

She shoves the paper back at James's chest, unable to contain her anger. James snatches the paper and puts it in his mouth, swallowing it whole and right at that moment, three loud bangs come at the front door.

"James! It's time to move!" yells Matthews from outside.
They stare at each other as James places a finger over his closed lips.

Sybil sets her jaw.

"Just get dressed," he whispers.

They finish putting on their clothes and meet Matthews and his companions outside. James, Sybil and Matthews make their way to the rocket, while the rest of the leadership members pile into the tanks and other military vehicles on the property.

As they take off in the shuttle, James holds Sybils hand tightly. He gives it a squeeze. James used to do this all the time as a way to tell Sybil that he loved her nonverbally. She would usually squeeze back, but this time, she does not. He squeezes again, but harder this time as he runs his thumb on the back of her hand. Sybil reluctantly gives a soft squeeze back.

Matthews is looking at them. Smirking.

"Writing a speech?" Matthew's asks.

"What?" replies James.

"Unless this is some new fashion statement, you've got a pencil on your ear."

James reaches up to his ear and snatches the pencil.

"Right. Ha. I must have forgotten it up there," he says. "Thanks."

Matthews scoffs and looks out the window.

Today's rally is taking place at an old football stadium where the New York Giants used to play. That was before the NFL, and all professional sports, were removed from society permanently. Useless distractions, Leadership said at the time, as all sports were considered dangerous and unnecessary and only led to violence and overpaid meatheads that abused their wives.

The rocket slows down and begins to descend to the landing pad a few feet below. The door opens and they are greeted by six men in Leadership uniforms.

"James, you will go with Matthews to the Leadership section and Sybil, you will come with us," one of them says.

Sybil looks at James with pleading eyes.

"Go on, love, I'll be with you shortly," James says, trying to provide reassurance as he releases his grip on her hand. Sybil reluctantly lets go before they are both guided off in separate directions at the side of the stadium. Helpless.

James and Matthews make their way around the stadium and onto the field. They are a bit early as citizens of the general public won't start showing up for another half hour.

"We'll find your seat over here," says Matthews as he motions over to a brilliantly set-up box that stands at one end of the field. "We wanted you to have a nice view of the stage," he says chuckling.

The box is extensively wide and spans from one end of the endzone to the other. It is two stories tall with pearly white painted finishes and a black trimmed border. There are silver stairs stationed in the middle of the apparatus that are guarded by two-armed Leadership members.

As they ascend the stairs and enter the Box, they meet multiple Leadership members from James's division. They are tasked with setting up food and drink and are moving like worker bees in a hive.

"Hey there, friend! Come on in and help us set this up," says Eric.

"Well, I'll leave you to it," says Matthews as he pats James on the back and begins to leave. "Enjoy the show."

"We got burgers and dogs, and all kinds of imported beer!" Eric gushes. He motions to a stack of chairs. "Give me a hand?"

James goes over and grabs a chair from the top of the stack and places it at one of the tables. Some of the other members from his division are setting plates and cutlery down on the tables while others are tasked with fixing the décor of the surrounding environment. But James just continues to stand there. He freezes as all he can think about is Sybil's impending doom. Huge windows spread horizontally throughout the enclosure, providing an excellent view of the field where a stage is being set up. James glances out the window and looks for Sybil. There is no sight of her. Beads of sweat traverse his forehead. He feels the inside of his shirt become uncomfortably moist and hot. His stomach is in knots.

"You're gonna make me do all the work, huh?" asks Eric as he grunts while lifting a stack of chairs. "Quit daydreaming and help me, friend."

"Right, sorry," says James as he goes to grab another chair.

"I remember how hard this day was for me," says Eric. "Just keep your mind busy. That's my advice. It will be over soon."

"Wait, what do you mean? Why did you say that?"

"Oh, they do this with all the new guys. I had a wife before all this, believe it or not. We do what's necessary to be where we are. You'll see."

James thinks carefully about his next words as he sits down at the table. He bounces his leg and tries to temper his mind. No use. He rises from his chair and approaches Eric.

"This isn't actually going to happen, right?"

"Hey. Woah there, friend. Let's back it up!" barks Eric as he places his hands on James's shoulders. "You need to get your shit together buddy- like now. He whispers. What's done is done, that's it, say goodbye, it's over."

"But Eric-"

"Pick up that chair and keep quiet if you know what's good for you. This is your chance to prove your loyalty."

The rest of the Leadership members begin filing into the watch box, piling their plates with food from the buffet. Their cups overflow with fine imported ale. It is clear that the rally is getting ready to start as the stage is now fully set up and thousands of people begin to surround the stadium. Spectators wave flags and banners. They look like ravenous dogs waiting to be fed.

Then, the gates open.

Over 80,000 members of the General Public begin to pack the stadium seating until it is full. Regiment tanks drive on the field with their blasters pointed to the sky. New Haven flags and power symbols hang from every wall. Hundreds of armed Leadership members are stationed at every intersection of the stadium and throughout the field.

On the stage, ten prisoners stand on large blue buckets with nooses around their necks, gags in their mouths, and bags over their faces. Several Leadership members stand on each side of the prisoners, all armed with high powered submachine guns. As the people shuffle in and pack the stands and the field, the New Haven fight song begins to play. The crowd sings in harmony.

James, Eric, and around twenty other members of Leadership sit idly in the watch box singing along. James can hardly function as he wonders if Sybil is one of the prisoners with a bag over her face.

Maybe this is just another simulation.

He sits there with his head in his lap, and his hands over his eyes as he peeks through the gaps between his fingers.

"Cheer up James, the show's about to start!" Eric says as he takes a seat next to him.

James only sucks in some air.

A moment later, a rocket can be seen approaching from the sky. This one is bright blue and larger than the others James has seen. New Haven is printed on the side of the rocket in big and bolded font along with the words:

I live for you, and you live for me.

Its monstrous size looks unreal as it descends as gingerly and carefully as a well-trained gymnast. As it lands on the pad, the crowd goes berserk. The door opens as smoke and gas releases from the rocket's engines. The Woman appears through the smoke, arriving to loud cheers and applause as she makes her way across the stage. She is wearing a blue pantsuit with jet black trim along the border. This matches her rocket perfectly. Her blonde hair looks flawless and buoyant as it bounces with her strides. Her cheeks are blushed, and they complement her ever-so animated smile.

She grabs the microphone that stands alone next to the prisoners and takes a minute to bask in the applause.

"Good morning New Haven!" she exclaims to the crowd.

"Welcome all to your weekend Rally! Today we have ten filthy cockroaches to be flushed. These ten prisoners were caught planning an overthrow of your great country. The most heinous of crimes. The most unforgiving of actions. What great shame they bring to their families and to you, their neighbors!"

The crowd boos and hisses, hurling insults at the condemned.

"Today, these ten betrayers of our cause, will face the ultimate judgment. You see, it is you who truly run our great nation!" she says, pointing to the crowd and pacing around the stage.

"It is you, the great people of New Haven, that possess all of the control and power that there is to be had. The power to see that the things happening here in our country are good and that these perpetrators are brought to justice! Shall we allow this civil unrest to continue?" She asks, her lips quivering with rage as the crowd booms with noise and anger.

"Shall we allow this utterly contagious contempt to run rampant throughout our state? Unobstructed?"

Again, the crowd roars.

"Then I say to you, great people of New Haven. Today justice will indeed be done! Leadership, reveal their faces!"

At this command, all of the bags are ripped off the prisoners' faces. One by one. Revealing ten terrified and horribly confused individuals—Sybil among them.

James swallows hard. He knows there is no plot to overthrow New Haven. He knows there are no traitors. Just ten people in the wrong place at the wrong time. Ten people that serve as an example to keep the citizens in line and underfoot.

The Woman marches over to Sybil. She shoves the microphone in her face and removes her gag.

"What last words do you have to the great people of New Haven that you have chosen to betray?"

"I am innocent, I swear it! Yells Sybil.

The crowd laughs.

"Help! James, where are you? Please!" Sybil's eyes dart helplessly. She is like a fish out of water.

James can no longer bear it. He stands up and walks to the end of the room, turning his back on Sybil for the final time.

"I have done nothing wrong, I would never plot against our country, I never would! This woman is evil! She's manipulating our minds and—"

The Woman whips the microphone away from Sybil's lips and places the gag back over Sybil's mouth. She tilts her head back as she lets out a bellowing laugh to the crowd. "In this traitor's last moments alive, she chooses to LIE to all of you. She knows she is guilty and yet cannot take ANY accountability for her actions. How pitiful," she says to the crowd as she turns her attention back directly to Sybil.

"You are going to die now. The time has come for-"

BOOM! BOOM! BOOM!

Just then, three enormous explosions to the left of the stage go off as everyone in attendance is stunned. The noise is so loud and disorienting that it is hard to tell exactly what is happening. But then, a section of the crowd near the stage starts to panic. They can see many members of leadership bleeding on the floor with large, open, and fatal wounds.

"Everyone! Please! Be calm!" instructs The Woman as Leadership readies their weapons.

A loud screech ripples through the stadium as the stage starts to collapse from damage. And then, another explosive goes off.

BOOM!

Then another.

BOOM!

Then two more across the field.

BOOM... BOOM.

Panic spreads throughout the stadium like wildfire as machinegun fire bursts forth from various individuals in the crowd. Leadership members are dropping like flies as bullets riddle their bodies and take off their heads. Stampedes of people are frenzied, trying to escape the explosions and gunfire of the ensuing civil war.

The Woman runs off the stage directed by her security detail, while the ten prisoners remain atop the buckets, unable to free themselves.

As guards escort the Woman back to her rocket, her security director, Barlow, grabs her by the arm and moves her to an area just below the stage. He instructs the rest of her detail to stay back and fight off the rebels. The Woman and Barlow slide into cover as the air fills with the screams of murder and droplets of blood.

"I'll keep you safe here," he says.

The Woman is still reorienting herself from the multiple blasts that violently shook her mind. She hunkers down on the floor and wipes the dirt from her face, as she comes to the realization that New Haven is under attack.

Staccato gunfire echoes throughout the stadium as the shells from hundreds of magazines litter the floor.

"What the fuck is going on? Is this internal or foreign?" she asks.

"Internal," he says as he walks around her peering out through the holes of the encampment.

"Shit. I had a feeling. How do you know?" she asks.

Barlow takes his eyes away from the holes in the wood and crouches beside her.

"New Haven is done," he says as he produces a knife and slides it across The Woman's throat.

Blood spurts forth. She falls back, choking on her own blood.

Her eyes go dark, and Barlow watches her soul leave her body.

He picks up his rifle and marches up the stairs out of the safe space and observes the anarchy taking place before him. He sets up on a perch and puts the rifle's scope to his eye. One by one, he takes shots at any leadership member that he can place within his crosshairs.

***

In the watch box, chaos ensues as explosions detonate randomly outside. Eric sprints over to a closet in the corner of the room. All the other Leadership members in the watch box are frozen in their chairs. James feels his heart in his throat.

Eric opens the closet revealing numerous rifles hanging by their straps.

"Everyone, get over here now and grab a rifle!" he demands.

All at once, the Leadership members hurry over to Eric. They form a line in front of him as he hands out the weapons one by one. James is still in his seat trying to figure out what side he is actually on.

"James!" yells Eric from the closet. "What the fuck are you doing?"

James stands up quickly and rushes over to Eric. "Sorry I-"

A rifle is pushed into his chest as Eric glares at him.

"Stay with me."

Leadership members hurl from the watch box as they run and duck for cover.

"James! Let's go!" yells Eric, as the two of them march through the gunfire, explosions, and field of innumerable bodies.

Just then, a voice is heard echoing throughout the stadium. "This is the revolution motherfuckers! We will stand for tyranny no more!" James looks up at the stage and sees a dark-haired woman yelling into the microphone. She is holding a submachine gun in the air, shaking it up and down as she speaks. Behind her is a group of masked individuals that are working to free the prisoners.

"Oh, fuck I think I know her," says Eric frantically, as he and James take cover behind a tank. "That's Aliya, she works at The Fund. With your wife!"

James doesn't respond. He is breathing heavily, trying not to cough from the clouds of smoke that surrounds them. James is frightened and his heart is beating out of his chest. He has never been in a fight before, let alone a coup. He doesn't even know how to shoot a gun. Yet here he is, hidden behind a tank, fighting an unknown enemy, holding a high-powered rifle in the midst of death and explosions.

"Formations!" yells a Leadership member. "Get in formations!"

"Formations?" James asks as gunfire ricochets off the tank's armor. "What the fuck is a formation?"

New Haven military and Leadership members get into their vehicles and trample over fleeing citizens. The Regiment's available army surrounds the stadium and closes in, shooting anyone who looks to be a part of this revolution. Eric positions his rifle over the side of one of the tanks and fires blindly at what he believes to be the positions of the opposition. The recoil is fierce and bumps Eric back with every round released from the barrel.

He empties an entire clip at the field of people, then withdraws his weapon and reloads. James grips his weapon close to his chest as explosions continue to go off around them.

BOOM... BOOM!

"James! Start shooting, damnit!"

James is frozen as he just sits in place, tightly gripping his rifle.

Eric scoots over to James and slaps him hard across the face. "Get it together if you don't want to die!" He positions James's hands in the proper way to hold the weapon. "Look over that side of the tank and help me kill these fuckers!"

James shakes his head and scoots his back up against the tank as he begins to peak over the side at the battle. Suddenly, a stray bullet hits the tank and bounces off 6 inches from his face, prompting him to retreat behind the tank again. He takes a deep breath through his mouth and closes his eyes. He opens them after a moment and looks over at Eric who is firing away, his lips curling with ferocity. Every muscle in James's upper body contracts as he holds a death grip on to the high-powered firearm. James scoots back up against the tank again and peers over the side. He sees Matthews about fifty yards away crawling to a corner with his legs as stiff as a light pole. Matthews has been shot a few times in the spine rendering the bottom half of his body paralyzed. Matthews is dragging the full weight of his body across the floor using only his hands. He finally makes it to the corner and sits up against a wall as he starts to tie a tourniquet around his leg.

"Oh shit! It's Matthews!" James exclaims with panic in his voice. "He's para-, he got-, he needs our help!"

"Go get him! I'll cover you," replies Eric, as he reloads his weapon.

James struggles to breathe. He remembers the man on the TV in the lunchroom; Martin Melnick.

What bravery he had. Going to another country like that.

He remembers how Martin was so well regarded by the news outlets. A real hero. James finds a hit of courage and counts to three before standing up and racing to Matthews. He runs with his weapon at the ready and fires some shots into the crowd around him not caring who he hits.

Bullets riddle the crowd as Leadership members start to get a hold on the conflict. They outnumber the rebel party four to one. As James runs to Matthews, he looks over at the stage for Sybil. She and the other captives huddle with the rebel party.

"Sybil!" he screams trying his best to get her attention as he runs. The noise of the battle easily drowns his cries.

Well, she looks safe enough up there.

He turns his attention to Matthews who is now only 20 yards away. James is hustling over as rounds of ammunition fly by and over him. He ducks his head and raises his arms as he narrowly avoids being hit by stray bullets. He's just ten yards out now. James raises his head and sees a rebel approaching Matthews with a knife. The rebel finds Matthews hiding in the corner and sticks a knife through his brain.

"Oh, god!" James yells as he slides behind an overturned military vehicle. Bullets continue to fly chaotically around him. The rebel pulls the knife out of Matthews's skull and leaves his limp body there on the floor.

"Fuck!" James screams scanning the carnage.

Before he can get his bearings, he feels a huge blow against his side. A powerful force takes him straight to the ground. He is tackled by another rebel that charged him from behind. They struggle back and forth as James's weapon is forced away from him to the floor. Now they're both unarmed. The rebel wraps his hands tightly around James's throat and straddles him in full mount position. His dirty thumbs imprint themselves into James's trachea as he gasps desperately for air. James focuses solely on the rebel's face. His eyes are bloodshot. His nose is scrunched. He has blood dripping from his face and onto his own.

This is it. I'm going to die.

The rebel uses every muscle and tendon in his hands to exert sharp pressure around James's throat. James throws soft punches at the rebel, but it's futile as the strength in James's body is being squeezed out of him. Tiny dots appear in his vision. Then, the force is gone.

Eric smashes the rebel over the head with the butt of his gun. James coughs violently and gasps for air as he is dragged to safety. Rocks and debris from the ground lacerate his back. James feels his perception come back to him as Eric leaves to go fire back at the rebels.

The battle rages on, and James is lying on the floor trying to catch his breath. He lays there for a while as the sounds of battle begin to fade. Dirt covers his face. Dust and blood envelop his hair like a thick and sappy shampoo. Blisters bulge on his fingers from the friction of the metal rifle. James's legs feel like they may crumble under his weight were he to try and stand. He sits up and begins to survey his surroundings. His lungs become engulfed with the smoke of detonated bombs and the ashy remnants of the bones of men. Most of the rebels are taking their last breaths. The mission to overthrow The Regiment and Leadership is failing. James sits down on the cold and hardened ground and watches as the few surviving rebels are taken into custody by Leadership, most of them barely clinging to life.

James finally stands up and looks around frantically for Sybil amongst the chaos. It is clear some time has passed. The field is flooded with bodies as he scavenges for anyone that might still be alive. New Haven ambulances tear onto the field, their red and blue flashing lights illuminating the shattered landscape. Injured bodies and corpses are slowly loaded onto their trucks.

As the dust settles, the battlefield falls into eerie quiet. The screams and groans of excruciating pain that once dominated the sounds of the field have finally ceased. Occasional blasts from leadership rifles echo around the stadium as The Regiment completes executions of anyone still alive but on the wrong side of the conflict. Leadership members pick their way over the rubble and debris, closing the eyes of their fallen compatriots and stashing their weaponry in piles.

Leadership has won a great battle. But James knows as well as the sky is black, that the war is just beginning.

10 THERAPY

Three days after the revolution

James is called into an office at the Workplace that he has never visited before. The office belongs to Sargent Bradley Valentine– a fifty-two-year-old balding, overweight meathead, also considered New Leadership.

Valentine had climbed the ranks almost as quickly as James has. But he was able to reach a higher position than James, as he is now the most senior ranking official in The Workplace. There are even rumors that he is being considered or groomed for a much higher position in Leadership—especially after the blood bath that took place three days earlier freed up a few jobs. Valentine is often described as a shark in a pond of minnows. He is stern, even keeled, and notoriously ruthless.

"Take a seat," says Valentine as James enters his office. James sits down at one of the uncomfortable steel barred chairs in front of Valentine's desk.

James crosses over his legs and places his hands in his lap.

Valentine takes out a classic Styrofoam lunch box and opens it, revealing three hardboiled eggs. He takes one of the eggs out of the box and begins to peel it with his overgrown fingernails, maintaining sharp eye contact with James. He doesn't speak a word. The sounds of his fingernails piercing the shell of the egg are amplified by the deadly silence of the room. Each crack of the egg sends shockwaves through James' entire being. Valentine turns his attention to the egg. It is almost fully dissected now. He peels off the last bit of shell, leaving the remnants scattered on the table in front of him. He examines the egg carefully. Bringing it closer to his face, as the sour dairy filled aroma consumes the room.

James is watching this uncomfortable display in bewildering confusion. He doesn't know what to do with his hands as he fidgets away, moving his thumbs in circles around each other.

Valentine finally takes a bite out of the egg, seeming to bask in the uncomfortable aura that is clearly radiating from James. Valentine slurps as he bites, heeding no mind for manners. Then, as the last bite of the egg is swallowed, he looks briefly at James with a deadly stare before reaching into the box for the next egg.

Scratch... scratch... scratch...

Peel... peel... peel...

"Sir? You wanted to see me?" James prompts.

Valentine says nothing and continues to slowly peel the shell of the second egg. Grumbling and growling as he does it with flakes still attached to his lower lip.

"I can come back later if you'd like. I wouldn't want to disturb your—"

"I'm trying to figure out why the fuck I need you," says Valentine plainly, still sharply focused on his breakfast.

James wrinkles his brow. "Why you need me?"

"Yes. Why do I need you?" Valentine repeats, looking directly at James now as he stops peeling.

"Well sir, I am here to catch traitors- and- and I believe I've done a bit of a good job," says James proudly. He is clearly trying to exude some form of confidence and self-achievement but internally rages a battle of right versus wrong and James wonders which side he is on.

"Right. Right. Is that why your wife is a lying, treasonous, petulant whore?" says Valentine.

Before James can respond, he continues. "See, I'm trying to figure out what the fuck to do with her as well. The both of you seem more like a pair of headaches than anything else."

James finds himself in a familiar place of mind, confusion—should he vouch for her or not?

"Sybil, ugh... Sybil isn't against New Haven," said James. "I'm not sure how she got mixed up in all of this, but she isn't a traitor. Of that, I'm sure."

Valentine slurps down the second egg and lets out a monstrous belch. He sits back in his chair and growls to himself.

"I've taken your wife, James. I've taken her and placed her in rehabilitation therapy. I've done this over the course of this interaction. All without lifting a finger! We'll keep her a few days and then she'll be released back into the wild as a better, more compliant person. A better citizen. A better wife."

James breathes a sigh of relief at the notion that Sybil won't be executed but he has no idea what rehabilitation therapy entails.

"Rehabilitation huh," says James as he ponders quietly to himself. "Ok, so she's there now? And she's safe? No one, will, like, hurt her?"

"She will be rehabilitated," barks Valentine. "As for you," he says, biting the third egg in his box as egg whites fall from his mouth to the desk, "you're on probation."

"Probation?"

"I've been doing this a long time now and I know a bad egg when I see one. I don't particularly like you. You're weird. Gauche and squirmy. Like a snake. I'm going to wait until you get feisty and lash out because that's gonna be the easiest way to cut off your head." Valentine points at his door. "Now get the fuck out of my office."

James gets up from his seat and approaches the door to leave. As he grips the handle and pulls it open, he begins to wonder if all the times that he has yearned for more in his life, and all the energy that that pursuit takes out of him, is worth it. He ponders if all the sacrifices that he's made over the last few years, at the expense of his marriage no less, are bearing him or his wife any fruit. His unquenchable thirst for power. For substance. For recognition. All that he ever really wanted. He wonders to himself if the juice is really worth the squeeze. He has lost Charlie, nearly his wife, but now, he senses that he is losing himself. What had Valentine done to earn his position anyways? Did he deserve to be where he is? Should they be on opposite sides of the desk?

He looks back at Valentine, who has shifted his attention to his work and pities him. Mostly because he knows that he is looking at his own reflection fast forwarded in time. He wonders if this is who he wants to become as he closes the door behind him and starts for his floor of The Workplace.

***

Thirty miles north in an abandoned warehouse, Sybil hangs naked upside down with her arms and legs tied together behind her back. She is blindfolded, alone, and freezing. Gravity is pushing all of the blood in her body directly into her head.

A door opens and someone walks into the space.

Click, clack.

Click, clack.

Click, clack.

Click, clack.

Silence.

Whack!

A large whip snaps across Sybil's back, striking bare skin and leaving a large laceration.

Sybil yelps in pain.

"Hello Sybil. I'm Morty!" says the man in a friendly tone of voice as he circles in front of her and removes her blindfold, smiling in her face. His sharply over whitened teeth sting her eyes.

Sybil focuses through her haze at the upside-down short and centrally bald man standing in front of her. She hawks up phlegm and spits it at his face.

Morty smiles, straightens, and wipes the spit from his brow.

"Mhmmm. Spicy! I like that." He walks over to the corner where a metal chair is stationed and drags it across the floor seating himself a few feet from Sybil. He crosses his legs and pulls out a notebook and pen from his jacket pocket as he drops the whip to the floor beside him. Morty uses both of his hands to push back the frizzy reddish hair that protrudes from the sides of his head.

"I am going to be your therapist, Sybil. And since we are going to get to know one another fairly intimately, I figured we could start with some pleasant introductions."

"Let me out of here!" Sybil screams as she tries desperately to free herself.

She is running out of energy and can feel the arteries in her head pulsating furiously as they become engorged with blood.

"Answer my questions and I'll untie you. It's as simple as that."

Sybil stops squirming for a moment. "Fine. I'm Sybil. Now fucking untie me."

"And I'm Morty!" he says as he waves his hands in the air like he is on stage giving a performance. "I'm pleased to meet you. Tell me, Sybil, what is your husband's name?"

"James Cleary."

"Great! That's correct!" He scribbles in his journal with a wrinkly and arthritic hand. "And what does Mr. Cleary do? Remember, the truth is ever-so important."

"Erm, uh, he works at The Workplace," says Sybil. "Can you please untie me? My head is starting to hurt."

"Was he involved in the plot that took place at the Weekend Rally?"

"No. He would never."

Morty picks up the whip and positions it in his hand as he looks at Sybil and stops writing.

"How long beforehand did you know that there was going to be a revolt at the weekend rally?"

Sybil stares at the whip in Morty's hand before answering. Morty still wears a wide smile on his face, as if he is a friendly neighbor asking about the weather.

"I- I never knew about any rev-"

SNAP

The whip comes flying across Sybil's abdomen with frightening speed and intensity. A harsh, sharp and stabbing pain shoots through Sybil's nervous system as she lets out a loud cry.

"Oh, dear, I apologize! That's a bit harder than intended," says Morty with a chuckle. "Sometimes, I'm amazed at my own strength!"

Sybil fights back tears but it's no use.

Morty takes a knife out from his pocket, revealing a sharpened blade. He walks slowly over to Sybil and shows her the point of the weapon. "Here, darling. Let me help you."

He uses the knife to slice through the rope that has Sybil dangling upside down, two feet above the floor. He slices vigorously back and forth until the rope is severed, and Sybil goes tumbling to the floor.

"There! That's much better, isn't it?"

Morty crouches and begins to dissect the rope that binds her hands and feet together. As she becomes unbound, he helps her to her feet and brushes the dust off her shoulders.

"How is that? Better?" he says, appearing to show genuine concern. "Oh no, please don't cry, dear. It gets me emotional."

"I'm fine."

"Great! You just stand there now, and we'll get back to the fun, fun questions!" he says as he sits back down in his chair. "Now, tell me what you know of this plot."

"I don't know of any plot, I swear. Listen to me, I've done nothing wrong."

The whip comes crashing down Sybil's chest. She reels to the floor, bleeding, the pain radiating from her core to her extremities.

"God! What do you want from me?"

"Sybil dear! I'm trying to help you. Don't you see that?" he says as he gets down to her level on the floor. He places one hand on Sybil's cheek as he attempts to console her. "I don't want to hurt you, Sybil. Please, you must believe that! I'm only after the truth. I know your husband told you about the plot. I just need to hear what it was that he told you. I'm on your side!"

Sybil remembers what James told her in the closet that morning. That he's going to help her and stop her from being executed. How could they possibly know about that? This is what Morty must be after.

"Morty, please. I don't know anything. James doesn't know anything. Please tell me why you think that we know something that we do not," Sybil says, jerking away from Morty's hand.

Morty retreats to his chair. He takes a deep breath and lets the air out in pieces as though meditating.

"At 5:43am Saturday morning, you and your husband were in the bedroom closet together. He left and grabbed a piece of newspaper and a pen. He came back to the closet around 5:45am where he likely wrote something down. I know that he told you he misses his parents or some garbage like that. But what I don't know, is what he wrote down on that piece of paper. Now my boss, Mr. Valentine, really, really, REALLY, wants to know what he wrote down on that piece of paper at 5:45am Saturday morning. Be a doll and tell us what is was so that we can all get back to our lives."

Sybil is stunned.

James was right.

"What are you fucking spying on us?" yells Sybil. "You put cameras in our house or something?"

SMACK

The whip runs across Sybil's face now sending her hurling to the floor once again.

"I am losing my patience Sybil. What is on the note?" he asks, not friendly anymore.

Sybil riles in pain as she thinks about what she should say.

"Yes! Yes! There is a note!" she says as she starts to giggle from the pain. "HAHAHAHA."

"What is so funny?"

Sybil continues to giggle as she holds a hand over her eye that is leaking a small amount of blood.

"What is so damn funny?"

Sybil continues laughing as the whip comes down on her with another frightening blow.

WHACK

"Tell me what the note says!" demands Morty.

Sybil is hysterically laughing now. Doing her best to stall as she thinks about what she could possibly say to keep herself and James out of more trouble. She believes James had rescued her from execution after all. The last thing Sybil wants to do in this moment, is to throw him under the bus.

"The note- the note ha-ha-ha," Sybil garbles, trying to talk through her tears and laughter. "It was his password to his PC account at the Fund! You fools! It was a fucking passcode!" She spits globules of blood on the floor and continues to laugh through her pain.

"A passcode. Really Sybil? Your husband randomly decides to write down his banking information as you get ready to leave for the rally?"

"Yes," Sybil replies. "It is as simple as that."

"Then what is it?"

"What is what?" replies Sybil.

"His fucking passcode."

Sybil pauses for a few seconds before speaking.

"3881-2465-4890*," she replies.

Morty sits back in his chair as he cross-references the code Sybil gives with the one on his tablet.

"Correct. All right, I'll bite. Tell me, why would he write his passcode down at such a random time and hand it to you like that? You see how that might be suspicious, don't you?"

"I do not care how it looks, that is what happened," says Sybil.

Morty folds his hands and leans forward. He stares at Sybil seriously before speaking. "This new guy, Valentine, he scares me. I mean he can be really mean. And he does not like your husband. Not. One. Bit."

"And?"

"Well darling, you may be widowed soon for all we know. What then? You need friends, Sybil. I can be a friend," he says pointing to himself with the hand that is still holding the whip.

Morty realizes he is still holding it and scoffs. "This whip, this warehouse, it means nothing," he says dropping the whip by his side. "We are just two people in two different circumstances really. You would be doing the same thing if the roles were reversed."

Sybil is sure at this point that she is dealing with a psychopath. She remains quiet for the time being as she is still trying to figure out what exactly Morty wants out of her.

"So, we are going to sit here for the next, oh- I dunno'- year or so, and rehabilitate you," he says making quotation marks in the air with his fingers and rolling his eyes.

"Year?" she asks sharply.

"Yes dear. If that's what it takes. Or would you rather I just shoot you in the face and we can be done?"

Sybil sets her jaw. "Right- so- what should I-"

"Oh, don't worry darling, I'm not going to hang you upside down again," he says laughing to himself. "I'm not sure why we still do that I mean really! Here, sit in my chair until I get back with some warm food. Yummy!" He rises and departs, leaving Sybil alone in the room.

Sybil sits down in the chair and tends to her wounds that are still bleeding and caked with dust and dirt from the unkempt floor. She tears a piece of her shirt and uses it to wrap around her abdominal wound which is the most severe of the three. Then, Sybil sits there for hours, completely alone with her thoughts until she falls asleep on the chair.

***

Sybil awakes suddenly to a bucket of freezing cold water that is splashed on her face by Morty.

"Rise and shine, princess!" he says, giving his usual creepy smile.

"Now get up. You're in my chair."

Sybil rises from the chair and stands back in her original position that she had when they first met. Morty plops down in the chair as he drops the whip on the ground and picks up a notebook from a plain grey briefcase.

"Ok, so I read all about you over the last few hours and wow I must say, bravo!"

Sybil widens her eyes but remains quiet. Her stomach turns and she tastes the acidic film of vomit on the back of her tongue.

"I mean a victim of sexual abuse, that's hard to go through love. You've come such a long way! Brava!" he says clapping his hands.

Sybil has not had to relive that part of her childhood in many years.

"I don't enjoy talking about that Morty," she says. Her eyes stern and laser focused.

"Well, I don't blame you, Sybil! I mean if you can't trust your own brother, ha-, I mean how do you know who you can trust at all, right?" Morty asks, as he stands from his chair and paces.

"Let me go, Morty. There's no reason for me to be here. I promise I- I'll go back to my normal life and- and- I won't say anything. I swear it."

"I will let you go when I feel that you are ready Sybil. I need something from you. Don't you see? I need something to give to Valentine, or I'm afraid what he'll do to me! You've gotta help me, Sybil. Please! We can help each other now. You tell me how they planned the coup. How your husband was involved, what was really on the note, ALL OF IT, and I'll let you go free! Without any more pain, no more whip, no more questions, nothing. You're free as a bird Sybil! Spread your wings!" he says joyously as he laughs to himself. "Or I'm afraid of what might happen…. To us."

Sybil looks hard at Morty. She studies his face as he maintains his flamboyantly histrionic expression. She presses her lips together and looks down before meeting his eyes once again.

"I heard rumblings about the executions the day earlier when I was at the Fund. I heard the executions were going to happen and that I might be a part of it. I also heard that it might be stopped but I wasn't given any details I swear."

"Go on," says Morty as he begins writing in his book.

"I was working my shift as usual when my new intern, Missy, pulled me aside and she— she told me everything. She said— something like, at the rally, you won't be in any real danger. She told me not to worry and that everything would be fine. I didn't know what she meant by any of it, but when I read the paper that morning, it all started to make sense."

Morty nods and continues writing. He flaps the fingers of his free hand, motioning for Sybil to continue.

"James never knew of any plot. He wasn't involved at all. You must believe me. I actually think James thought that HE might be executed or something and that's why he wrote down his code. So that I could access his excess funds or something- I'm not sure. But that's the truth."

Morty snaps his notebook shut. "Thank you, Sybil. This is good information." He rises.

"Wait! Where are you going? Am I going to get out of here?"

Morty turns, the smile gone from his face. "Eventually."

Sybil sits down on the dust-filled floor and listens as Morty's footsteps get quieter and quieter as he exits the building. She is left alone again there in silence.

Sybil immediately feels regret for Missy, but she feels justified in her actions as her top priority is to keep herself and her darling husband alive.

"It was the only way," she says softly to herself as she twiddles her thumbs.

Hours go by, and Sybil spends that night on the cold dark floor of the warehouse. The one exit door is bolted shut and the rest of the warehouse is surrounded by concrete walls with no windows. She notices a faint hint of light as it peaks through the small crack in the door. A few slim and whisking rays kiss the hardened floor. Sybil watches as they fade over time. She figures she can either wait for Morty to come back eventually or she can hang herself using the chair and the rope that were so cleverly left behind. She chooses the former.

Hours pass and the sun starts to rise again. Morty enters the door and Sybil's rehabilitation truly begins.

"Rise and shine my dear! Rise and shine."

Sybil groans and rubs her eyes awake. "Good morning Morty. Just the man I was hoping to see."

"It's time for history class. Do you enjoy history?"

"No."

"Wonderful," he says clearing his throat. "Now. New Haven has been blessed with such a rich and colorful history. Especially for a country at such a young age! We have been fortunate enough to be able to identify traitors before they cause problems and deal with them. That is part of what makes our history so great!"

Sybil thinks back to her being identified as a traitor. Those baseless accusations. The wrap over her head. The gag in her mouth. The screaming of the crowd. What problems did they think she was going to cause?

"I am going to read you a list of names of previous traitors, and I want you to memorize and repeat back to me these names, as well as the charges that were brought against them. Do you think you can do that?"

"Well yeah, but-"

"Excellent," he says, cutting her off.

Morty holds a large square tablet. He scans the screen and begins to read down the list.

"Rachel Parks- accused of treason against New Haven and executed for forging documents in an effort to escape to another country and provide them our military secrets."

"Leslie Burg- accused of treason against New Haven and executed for trying to assassinate a Leadership member with poison."

"Jacob Ferris- accused of treason against New Haven and executed for trying to smuggle his wife Anita out of the country to trade military secrets with a foreign enemy."

"Now you go ahead," he says, looking straight at her with expecting eyes.

Sybil hesitates. "So, you want me to repeat all of that? Everything that you just said?"

"Precisely."

"Alright then. Rachel Burg, she forged some… documents. Leslie uh, Burg. No wait. Park. No, was it Burg? Leslie…"

Morty sighs. Allow me to repeat myself. He looks down at the tablet to read again.

"Rachel Parks- accused of treason against New Haven and executed for forging documents in an effort to escape to another country and provide them our military secrets."

Sybil's eyes widen. "Right, Parks. Rachel Parks. Ah, I said Burg, didn't I?"

"Yes…"

This goes on for days. Continuous trial and error of reciting the traitor's names and what they were executed for. When she says them incorrectly or even mispronounces a name, she is made to start over from the beginning. Morty says this is because everyone should always know what happens to the traitors. Their names, their crimes, and what punishments they receive for their wrongdoings. He says this will help dissuade future treasonous thoughts or actions because their deaths are always readily on the minds of the general public.

Morty provides some food occasionally for Sybil. A piece of crusty bread here and there, a bottle of water on occasion. But he always keeps her just hungry enough so that she will continue with the rehabilitation games in exchange for food. His one intention is the reshaping of her mind, but Sybil is growing excessively fatigued.

"We are going to play another little game," says Morty.

"We are going to play another little game," Sybil repeats. Her words are dry and emotionless. She's exhausted from days of mental exercises and little food or hydration.

"This game is called Guess the Lie," he says enthusiastically, prancing around in a circle. "I am going to make five statements and I want you to tell me which one of them is false. Remember Sybil. Only one can be false. Are you ready to play?" he asks as he looks down at his notebook.

"I am ready to play."

Great! Alright. Statement number one," he says before he clears his throat. "Your favorite color is pink," he looks up from his notebook to observe Sybil's reaction to the statement. She remains staring straight ahead. Blank faced. Waiting for the rest of the statements to be read before reacting. Morty smiles and looks down at his notes.

"Statement number two. You know The Regiment knows what is best for you," he looks up from his notebook. Sybil doesn't flinch.

"Statement number three. You understand that the word of Leadership is truth," he looks up again.

"Statement number 4. Your sexual desires are being fully realized in this environment," he pauses but doesn't look up this time.

"Statement number 5. You love your country."

Morty looks up from his notebook and waits for Sybil to speak. She continues staring straight ahead but her eyebrows are turned down slightly.

"Guess," he says firmly.

"Statement number one is false," she says. "My favorite color is green."

Morty produces a bell from his pocket and swings it back and forth. The shrill sound of the bell stings Sybil's ears. She shudders.

"Well done darling!" he says as he reveals a large piece of bread in his hand. Sybils eyes start to water at the sight. She is starving and knows it's entirely obvious, but she doesn't care. Morty tears off a small piece of the bread and leans forward to offer it to Sybil.

"Go on," he says.

She stares at the bread for a moment. She wants so badly to refuse. To show Morty that she doesn't need his hand outs. That she is strong enough to endure whatever torture or rehabilitation he can throw at her. But Sybil understands the psychology of the situation. She understands that the sooner she plays along, the sooner she will be free. She understands that if she can just convince Morty that he's changed her as a person, she can get back to James. Back to safety. She reaches out and reluctantly takes the piece of bread.

"That's a good girl," Morty says as the sides of his mouth shift upwards. "Time for round two."

After a few days of these games, Morty releases Sybil. She appears as a confused, and lost version of her former self. Morty now believes that Sybil is not the same woman she was when she was taken. Now, she is a more compliant person, a better citizen, a better wife.

11 DEATH

Sybil walks through the front door of her home to find James nervously preparing food in the kitchen. She kicks off her shoes and closes the door behind her. James hears the door and turns around.

"There you are," he says rushing over to her. "I was beginning to worry."

"It was only a few days," she says, trying to withhold her emotions.

James wraps his arms around her, and she falls heavily into his chest. His hold, irresistible. She begins to sob as he runs his hands through her hair.

"It's alright my love. It's going to be alright."

"I'm just glad to be home," she says sniffling and wiping her teary eyes.

James continues holding her tightly and shakes his head. "What did they do to you?"

"Nothing. We just- I…"

Sybil looks around the room conspicuously. "I'm so hungry," she blurts out. Her eyes peak from behind his shoulder. "What on earth are you attempting to cook over there?"

James laughs to himself as he turns around to his unorganized mess of vegetables that flood the marble countertops. "Well, it seems we got extra vegetables in our food supply this week. I was just trying to figure out if I'm supposed to cut these carrots horizontally or vertically."

Various pieces of carrots and asparagus all sliced at different lengths and angles are piled on top of each other. Sybil sees this and laughter replaces her tears.

"Please for the love of god. Let me help you," she says giggling. "Please remove your apron and step away from the vegetables."

"At once," says James as he happily removes the apron from his head.

***

The next day, Sybil returns to her job at The Fund. She hurries up the golden stairs, brushes through the wide double doors, hangs her coat, and proceeds to her station. Missy is there to greet her.

"Good morning, ma'am. Bright day ahead!" Missy says with a wide inviting smile.

Sybil nearly chokes with guilt but continues walking past her without saying a single word. She wonders if anyone will question her absence. They don't.

Sybil plops down in her chair and begins to nervously straighten out the various books and loose paper on her desk when Missy appears behind her.

"I can do that for you ma'am, not to worry. Your first appointment is waiting for you at the booth."

"Sorry I'm a bit out of sorts this morning," says Sybil.

Missy just stands there smiling.

Sybil leaves to greet her first customer while Missy stays behind to organize Sybil's desk. As she begins to place loose papers in a filing bin, she stops for a moment. She notices that Julie, a concierge attendant, is staring at her from the doorway of The Fund. She places the papers down and peers out the window of Sybil's office to get a better view. Julie stands with a few members of Leadership, their gazes fixed on Missy. She smiles as the men start walking toward her with Julie looking on from behind them. Missy exits the office and meets the three Leadership members in the adjoining hall.

"Hello gentlemen. How can I help you?" she asks.

"Melissa Anderson?".

"Yes, that's me."

"You are under arrest for Treason against New Haven."

The men grab Missy by her arms as she squirms and squeals in confusion.

"Wait, what? I don't know what you're talking about! Please! Let me go!"

Onlookers and staff watch in helpless silence. As Sybil rounds the corner, she locks eyes with Missy. Missy reaches out her hand as the Leadership members guide her away.

***

Four blocks to the north, James is at his desk reviewing leads on potential treasonous activities in New Haven. He is tasked with reviewing these leads and assigning them to an underling for investigation. He picks up a file from the stack on his desk when Samuel knocks repeatedly on his office door.

"Come in."

Sam enters the office in a huff and out of breath—not unusual for a man of his girth.

"I've got him, sir. I've got him!" Sam wheezes.

James furrows his brow. "Who?"

"I finally nailed one, sir!"

"That's great Sam, but I'm still not sure what you're talking about. Who did you… nail?"

"Right, sorry. So, I've been tracking that one guy you were telling me about. The one with the fancy hair."

James tilts his head. "The one with the fancy hair?"

"Yeah! That's the one!"

James palms his forehead. "And?"

"Right, well the fancy hair man is going to be meeting the rest of those plotters tonight at an address I wrote down... somewhere..." he says, patting his pockets. "I tapped their entire conversation! What fools!"

"Well, that's great Sam. Well done," James says. "Why don't you gather the rest of squad B and we'll meet in the War Room in fifteen minutes to go over the details."

"On it!" Sam says, as he trudges out of the office.

Fifteen minutes later, James meets the rest of Squad B in the War Room. The room's walls are painted blood red and sport multiple screens and mirrors that alternate in decorative patterns. High-tech tracking devices are stationed in the corners next to piles of unopened cardboard boxes. Various military portraits and New Haven banners surround one brilliant oversized wooden table that lies in the center of the room. It gleams of the finest white oak.

There are twenty-six squads total in The Workplace. They are each named after a letter of the alphabet, and each contain four members strategically placed together based on their individual personalities. They work together on tasks to bring traitors to justice and find clues regarding potential overthrow plots. They are essentially tasked with keeping New Haven safe. James is in charge of squad B which includes Sam, Harry, Arayah, and Cyrus.

Samuel's bubbly personality allows him to act as a decoy in situations that need a bit of… fluff. He is nearly 300 pounds and dresses like a bell boy.

Harry is the smart one. He's exceptionally tall and lanky and wears black studded earrings with points on the ends. He's dressed in a fully buttoned button-down shirt that practically chokes him at the neck. He's responsible for planning the sting operations down to every minute detail and making sure that everyone knows their roles.

Arayah is the brawn and muscle of the group. He's a trigger happy, beefy, 27-year-old with God-given physical talent and ability. He's an excellent wrestler with a propensity for violence. Arayah is insecure about his height and tends to take out his frustrations in combat by being unapologetically ruthless.

Lastly, there's Cyrus Bell, whom the rest of the group refers to as Mr. Luck. Cyrus always seems to know when the best time to launch a bust would be. He is an intelligence wizard and knows where everyone of interest is at all times. He does this by monitoring their every move using an algorithm that he created and coded into the computing system. He is a bright and budding star in the field of catching traitors and seems to be followed by good fortune.

James sits at the head of the table in the War Room as the rest of Squad B finds their seats in attention.

"So, it seems we've got a bit more than a bite this time on Marcus. Eh,

Sam?" says James.

"Yes sir!" Sam says. "We've got ourselves a location and I know it's going down tonight. I just don't know at exactly what time. I overheard most of their conversation and they were talking about explosives, and weapons, and the great revolution, blah-blah-blah."

"What is the precise location?" Harry asks, producing a tablet from his pocket. "We'll have to be careful about the surrounding area so that we don't tip them off on entry."

Sam starts to fumble with some papers from his notebook. "Uh- ok- here it is- right. It's seven one five my-rah straunt."

"My-rah straunt?" James says. "What the fuck is that?"

There's a beat of silence in the room.

"It's my restaurant," Arayah says rolling his eyes. "Dumb-ass."

"Oh, his restaurant. I know where that is!" Cyrus says. "He owns the Italian place across the street from the park. And the seven one five is probably the meeting time Sam, like 7:15. That was a nice try though!" he says patting Sam on the back.

"Wait. Marcus owns Agucci's?" says Sam. "Well then who's going to take over if he goes down for treason? I love their garlic rolls and I just earned my restaurant privileges!"

"Well, we wouldn't want you to miss any garlic rolls, now would we?" says Arayah.

"Guys, pay attention. Here's what we're going to do," Harry says. "Everyone is going to meet out front of the workplace at 6:45pm sharp. I'll have the route were taking picked out, as well as the entry point. James, we're going to need something quiet for transport. Marcus likes to hang outside sometimes."

"The guns can be as loud as they want though, right?" Arayah asks smiling.

"Maybe we should let them have their meeting for a bit before we bust in. We wanna' make sure everyone is there," says Cyrus.

"Good point. Ok fine, we'll meet at seven and show up fashionably late," Harry says.

"Great. I'll get us, the vehicles, and weapons. I will uh- leave you all to discuss the plans of entry and you can fill me in this evening. Good work boys," James says as he leaves the room.

A few hours later, the clock strikes 7pm. James heads outside of The Workplace to meet Squad B who are already waiting for him. The sun is in the midst of setting and darkness is settling in.

James instructs the 4 men to follow him to the lot to get changed and equipped for the operation. The five of them put on Leadership sting suits which are all black and cover them from head to toe.

The sting suits are breathable and insulated to keep an ideal temperature stable. Their eyes are covered with light weight, fitted goggles that include heat sensors, night vision and Xray vision. They are each given an earpiece for communication during the mission.

James hands them each a Leadership special operations rifle. These rifles can switch between burst, semi-automatic, and automatic and can compress themselves into the size of a pistol. Each of them is also given an assortment of smoke grenades, frag grenades and stun grenades. The stun grenades are the newest innovation of the New Haven military. They work by exploding an electrical impulse that travels through the floor. It can shock anyone in a quarter-mile radius not wearing a sting suit.

James leads the crew to two vehicles called Stingers that are stationed right outside of The Workplace. The Stingers are sleek, coupe-like supercars that run on pure electricity. They're as quiet as a mouse and are specifically designed for stealthy operations. They are able to change colors to blend in with the surrounding environment like a chameleon. Stingers are armored with lead surfaces and bulletproof sleds which look kind of like traditional tires but are more elongated than round. Stingers can travel in any direction on a dime and are an absolute thrill to drive.

"Shotgun!" yells Sam.

James and Sam get into one Stinger, while Arayah, Cyrus and Harry pile into the other. James follows Arayah down a dark road right off of the main one. It's pitch black now and the road is quite bumpy. James looks down at the time.

7:18 pm

"We're just a couple of minutes away from Agucci's boss," Sam says.

James looks back at the road with Arayah's car ahead of him. He glances down at the camera displaying his rearview, confirming they are alone.

"Remember, boys," James says, pushing his earpiece. "We want these fuckers alive. Especially Marcus. Don't pull the trigger if you don't have to. Got that, Arayah?"

"Yeah, yeah," says Arayah. "Just make sure Sam doesn't sit on him."

Sam hears this and smiles as he looks out the window.

A few minutes later the Stinger slows down to a stop behind an abandoned building across the street from Agucci's.

The squad exit their vehicles and coalesce behind the corner of the building whose towering height blocks the moon. A perfect blanket of dark cover shields them from pedestrian eyes across the street as their pitch-black stinger suits melt their presence into the scene. The lights from the restaurant illuminate a few figures who are standing at the front doors of Agucci's.

"Ok. It's go time. Everyone behind me for approach," James says.

The five men rally behind James as they prepare to advance further. They place their goggles over their eyes and switch-on the night vision setting. In linear fashion, they rush to the side of the building where they can get a better view of the entrance to the restaurant. There are six people outside of the front door talking, but even louder conversational noise can be heard coming from the restaurant every time the front doors open.

"I believe Marcus and the rest of them are downstairs," says Cyrus. "When you get into Agucci's, most people will be seated in the general dining room, but there's a downstairs hidden area that not a lot of people know about. That's where they'll be."

"How do we get past the general patrons?" Sam asks.

"Follow me," says Cyrus as he leads the group around the back of the restaurant where four trash chutes are stationed. Cyrus creeps over to one of the chutes and removes the lid.

"This one isn't a garbage chute," he says. "It's an emergency exit from the basement with rotating peristaltic panels. If we enter this way, they'll have nowhere to go."

"Are you sure?" whispers James. "We can't fuck this up."

"Oh, I'm sure. Trust me, this is the best way in. I'll go first. Everyone ready?"

James takes a deep breath and holds his weapon close to his chest. His fingers find a familiar position on the gun as flashes of the revolution flood his mind. The sight of Matthews getting stabbed through the brain is unshakable for a moment. But James orients himself. "Wait, let's hit 'em with a stun grenade first. That should make them easier to tackle."

"Great idea," Arayah says.

James holds open the lid as Arayah moves into position, gripping the grenade.

"Ok, on my mark," says James. "One… two… three!"

Arayah pulls the pin and tosses the stun grenade down the chute and into the basement where it tumbles and bounces off the walls of the chute and onto the floor. A moment passes and then the electrical impulse explodes.

"GO! GO! GO!" yells James, as the five of them jump into the chute, riding it down into the basement of the restaurant.

The basement is dimly lit by candles and torches, and the air is musty smelling of mold and fish. There are four round tables in the room with chairs all around and a body in each of them. All of which are men, mostly over the age of 45. These men are stunned where they sit and remain motionless. Their eyes are wide, and every muscle in their bodies is contracted to its fullest extent. Layers of clenched fists surround the tables.

"Everybody hit the fucking ground!" yells James, as Sam, Arayah, and Harry all point their weapons at the individuals at the tables. Nobody moves because they're physically unable to. They are frozen in place from the stun grenade. Arayah and Harry begin to push each one of them to the ground as they topple over, still stiff and contracted.

"Marcus Callowani, stand up now!" Arayah demands.

The bodies on the ground start to become relaxed as a few of them are able to sit up.

"I'm not going to ask again, Marcus!" says Arayah.

Tension fills the room as it becomes eerily quiet. James feels hot as a rage inside of him quickly reaching its boiling point.

"Marcus, stand the fuck up!" yells James as he frantically scans the room.

"I'm going to give you five seconds to come out before I start shooting," says Arayah.

Still no response. James shakes his head with frustration and pushes a table over on its side. "Cyrus and Sam, search the place!"

Cyrus and Sam make their way around the hostages and look for Marcus. The basement is set up like a small apartment with a living room, a bedroom, and a separate bathroom. Sam makes his way to the bedroom while Cyrus searches the bathroom.

Sam opens the door to the bedroom slowly with his rifle. A wooden bed frame holding a crusty mattress with white fitted sheets lies before him. But not Marcus. He enters the room and turns the corner, placing his back firm to the wall. Papers are scattered everywhere, and the room looks like it has been turned upside down. Sam begins to inch toward the closet. One foot in front of the other and breathing heavily. He approaches the closet door handle and reaches out his hand when-

BOOM, BOOM, BOOM!

The sound of three consecutive gunshots ring throughout the basement.

"He had a gun!" yells Cyrus as he back-pedals from the bathroom with splashes of blood stains on the front of his suit. "He- he had a gun!"

James rushes over to where Cyrus is standing and turns to investigate the bathroom. There, lie a middle-aged Italian man with beautifully slicked back dark hair. Slumped over the bathtub. Dead. With a shower curtain mangled and dangling in front of his bullet riddled body.

"What the fuck did you just do man?" James says.

"I- I thought he had a gun, I swear!"

"You shot him! We needed him for questioning, you idiot!"

"I'm sorry, it all happened so fast. I thought he was going to kill me!"

James turns red and stares at Cyrus with bloodshot eyes. "Well fuck Cyrus. Now we've got nothing. Nothing except a bunch of fucking hostages. God damnit!"

James feels rushes of insecurity. His cheeks are hot and his face burns with panic. Flourishes of fiery energy race through his body. He realizes he has lost control of the situation. He brushes by Cyrus and fires a shot from his firearm into the ceiling.

"Everybody better listen the fuck up! I am in charge here and I know what all you fuckers were planning here tonight. Who is going to come forward and tell me the truth? Huh?"

Silence.

James is now fuming with rage. "Alright fine. Whoever tells me the truth first, gets full immunity. You have thirty seconds before I take every one of you and put you in a fucking labor camp, until your hands bleed and your feet fall off!" James feels intoxicated by power and is proud of his ability to rattle off threats.

The hostages look around the room at each other. All seeing if anyone will come forward first.

"Twenty seconds left…"

Silence.

"Fifteen. Times running out"

Silence.

"Ten seconds until you're all fucked!"

Still nothing.

"Five…four…three…"

"Okay!" says a voice from the crowd. "Ok, fine! Yes, Marcus has a plan. Fine. Just please don't hurt us!"

Arayah identifies the man speaking, grabs him by the shirt, and drags him to the center of the room.

"Continue," Arayah says.

"He- he said we can get away. He said we can leave New Haven for good and that no one will ever know! We wouldn't have to hurt anyone or blow anything up. We can just leave."

James approaches the young man and kneels to his level so that they're eye to eye. He grabs the man's face and aggressively tilts it backward.

"What was your plan?" James asks.

"We were going to leave tomorrow night. All of us, we…"

Just then, one of the hostages appears behind Sam and places him in a chokehold, holding a revolver to his head. Sam shoots his hands up into the air and drops his weapon.

"Woah, woah, woah! What exactly do you think you're doing?" says Harry. "Let him go. Now. Let him go and no harm will come to you. You have my word."

The man is sweating furiously and gritting his teeth. "Your word? Your word ain't worth shit!" he says as he spits at Harry's feet. He presses the barrel of the gun deeper into Samuel's temple. Sam feels the cold metal imprinting into his skin and cringes.

"I want you all to leave now or I shoot this little piggy."

"Oh shit!" says Sam. "I don't think he's joking, guys!"

James draws his weapon and points it at the man holding Sam.

"You know that we can't do that," James says. "Just put the gun down, and we'll talk this out."

"Fuck you. I'm sick of leadership! I'm sick of New Haven. I'm sick of being told what to do and where to go. This isn't freedom. We're slaves and you're the devil. You're going to have to answer for what you've done. All of you! I- I can't live like this anymore!" The man swipes at angry tears.

"Hey! Wait, wait, wait. What's your name?" asks Harry.

James still points his weapon.

"No, I'm done talking."

BOOM

The man pulls the trigger and a bullet travels directly through Samuel's brain.

"No!" Arayah screams as he shoots back at the man before James can even process what just happened.

BOOM, BOOM, BOOM, BOOM, BOOM!

The man's body falls on top of Samuel's as chaos erupts in the room. The remaining hostages grab what they can off of the tables and throw candles, plates, forks, and knives at the squad. Anything that's within reach is thrown at will.

James ducks for cover behind an overturned chair as objects fly all around him. Arayah tackles a hostage and begins to beat him unconscious.

Harry and Arayah fire freely, killing multiple hostages as they fight for their lives. James is still taking cover from behind a chair. There are bodies all over the floor, most of them dead but two or three them roll in agony from their wounds. Harry is mounted on top of one last person when James gets up, rushes over and kicks Harry off him. The man is elderly and crying; he clearly does not want to fight. James looks down on the man with pity.

"You can rot in a cell for all your remaining years, or I can kill you. Here and now. You choose," he says, his hands trembling.

The man whimpers and moans.

James waits a moment before putting the barrel of his weapon to the old man's forehead. He pulls the trigger.

BANG

The crying stops.

James, Arayah, and Harry look around the room at all the bodies and blood. Their eyes land on Samuel's motionless corpse.

"Fucking hell," Arayah says softly as he pushes over a chair.

James gulps and runs his hand over his head. "Everybody, grab your shit. We're done here."

"Wait. We need a story," says Harry.

"I'll write a report. We encountered resistance and they all had guns or something and a fight broke out... I don't know. Fuck!" James said. "Just get in the stinger and let's go."

12 PILLARS OF A NEW WAY

James gets home late that night. He creaks open the front door so that he won't wake Sybil. He thinks that she's likely waiting up for him before giving up and going to bed as she's done so many times before. He takes off his shoes quietly, places down his bag, and starts for the bedroom. All of the lights in the house are off, as James tiptoes his way around on the creaking wooden floors.

He makes his way into the bathroom, turns on the shower and cries as the steam begins to engulf the bathroom. James is stiff and wiping away the tears from his eyes. He can't stop his mind from replaying the events over and over in his head. Images of Sam falling fatally to the floor. Arayah beating that man to death. Pulling the trigger and executing that poor elderly man.

James picks up Sybil's handheld mirror and stares at his reflection. He looks deeply into his own eyes and observes himself as a sad, weak and crying man. He pulls the mirror away and looks down at the floor. Ashamed.

After wallowing in the shower, he returns to the bedroom and grabs a pair of underwear as he notices that Sybil is not asleep in the bed. He flips the light switch and looks around the room. He is alone. He wanders over to the living room to see if she is on the couch. He remembers her sleeping there on late nights before. He flips the switch illuminating the room.

Nothing.

"Sybil? Where are you?"

There is no response.

James calls out to her as he paces around to the kitchen but stops as he finds a note on the dining table. It reads:

James, I've made a tough choice. I am running away with Cameron. Please, do not attempt to Find me. I do not recognize you anymore. You're not the man I fell in love with. You really hurt Me. I tried. Enjoy the money. I hope you find what you are looking for. Please, keep your compass North.

James can't help but grin for a moment before changing his face quickly to a frown. His hands shake as he places the paper down on the table. He looks around the room for bugs or cameras before aggressively slamming his fist down on the table.

"This is what you did!" he screams to the cameras, wherever they are, as he picks up the note and shakes it at the air. "This is your fault! It's your fault that she's gone!

James flies into a rage as he throws his clenched fists repeatedly into the walls of his kitchen. He snatches cups from the cabinet and throws them across the room. Glass shatters immediately upon impact. He screams louder as he proceeds to destroy his home. He appears angry and hurt, but no tears come to his eyes.

James lies down on the floor of the kitchen with the note laying over his face. Alone, cold and bloody from his anger.

"Maybe I'll just kill myself," he says softly, muffled by the paper over his mouth. He blows it off of his face as spit flies everywhere. "I have a gun in my drawer, you know! Yeah. Maybe I'll use it!" he sniffles and continues yelling. "It sure would put an end to all this bullshit! Or maybe I'll just disappear into nothingness. Nothingness must be better than this."

He lies there for several hours, marinating in every thought that comes and goes from his brain.

"I hope the cameras are watching," he says quietly to himself.

Time to set this whole thing up.

First daylight eventually peaks through the windows. The rays from the sun sting his tired eyes. James picks himself up off the floor, rushes into his office and begins furiously writing a document titled Pillars of a New Way.

In just a few hours, James crafts a forty-five-page manifesto, heavily detailing new domestic laws that he will propose to senior leadership for immediate approval; with a special emphasis on four new rules.

Pillars Of A New Way
1. Women must abide by a strict curfew of 7pm every evening with no exceptions.
2. When husbands are not with their wives, a member of leadership will be designated to chaperone her to and from work.

3. Husbands will have to agree before a wife can choose another lover.

4. Any deviation of these rules is subject to imprisonment or death.

James is manic with energy as he throws on his clothes and heads to The Workplace. He arrives at his floor from the slide and shoots into his office, manifesto in hand. He opens the top drawer, picks up the earpiece, and places it into his ear.

"Good morning, James," says Lester. "What can I do for you?"

"Yes! Good morning indeed. Look, I've got something brilliant to bring to your attention. Can we meet?"

"Yes, that shouldn't be a problem."

Great! I-"

"I have some time in a few days."

"A few days? No, no, no. Now!" demands James. "I need to meet now. And I need Valentine there as well. It's very important."

"Are you kidding me? You don't give me orders James."

"I- I'm not giving you orders. I-… right," he says, lowering his voice. "Sorry, but we must meet. Do you think you could set this up? I'd be very grateful."

Lester lets out a long sigh. "Floor 12 conference room in one hour."

The line clicks.

James removes his earpiece and sits back in his chair. He stands up and begins to pace around his office. He strokes his chin for a moment before opening the door to his office.

"Cyrus, in here now!"

Cyrus stops what he is working on and promptly shuffles into James's office. "What's up boss?"

"Listen closely. I've created a brilliant document which I've called Pillars Of A New Way. It's a new law you see and It's going to be great!" James says with exuberance.

Cyrus crinkles his nose. "That's... brilliant James. Well done. What kind of law?"

"Yes, here. Read it and tell me about your thoughts before my meeting in an hour," he says as he hands over the large stack of papers to Cyrus.

"Quite lengthy though, isn't it?"

"Yes."

"You said one hour?"

"That's right. So, you should get to work."

Cyrus hurries out of the office with the manifesto and sits down at his desk to begin reading. Arayah shoots a sideways look from the neighboring desk. James stands at the glass window of his office and stares impatiently at Cyrus as he reads. James cannot stop his foot from tapping on the floor as he is filled with endless anticipation.

As Cyrus continues reading, his mouth gets longer and longer. He places his hands on either side of his temples as he flips through the pages. Three minutes pass by and James has lost his patience.

"Cyrus get back in here!" he barks.

Cyrus reluctantly stands up from his seat and enters James's office again.

They stare at each other without speaking.

"Well. What did you think?" James asks.

"But- but sir I've hardly read the first-"

"But-but-but," James says, mocking Cyrus with a scrunched-up face. "You skimmed it right? Just tell me what you think!"

"Well, to be honest, sir, and with all due respect, what I was able to read... it's highly illegible."

"Illegible?"

"Yes. I can't seem to make out half of the words on here. Maybe try and type this up or something."

James paces around his office and stops abruptly after a few seconds of silence.

"Cyrus."

"Yes Mr. Cleary?"

"Why did you shoot that man?"

"What?"

"The one in the shower, with the hair. Marcus."

"Uh- I- I told you, I thought he had a gun."

"Yeah, but he didn't though; did he?"

"Look sir, I'm sorry about that. I'm really sorry about what happened; to Sam, to everyone. I know that's not how it was supposed to go."

Memories of that night suddenly flash through James's mind like a bad movie that he never wants to see again.

"Get out," James says with a cracked voice. "Out. I need to focus."

Cyrus leaves the office without hesitation and returns to his tiny desk. He sits back down and lets out a long sigh throwing his hands up in the air. He's trying to process what just took place.

"What in the fuckity fuck was that?" asks Arayah.

"He's lost his marbles," replies Cyrus, looking over at Sam's empty desk.

A few minutes later, James exits his office with his manifesto and proceeds to floor 12. He paces around the conference table as he waits for Lester and Valentine to arrive. Twenty more minutes go by, and he is still alone in the room. He places his manifesto down on the table and spreads the pages out on the table so that they cover the entire surface like a tablecloth. Then, the door opens, and Lester Prime walks through.

"Hello James. I see you've been... decorating," he says as he sits down in one of the chairs and moves various pieces of papers out of his way. As he sits down, Valentine appears at the door.

"Let's make this quick, gentlemen. What could possibly be so urgent?" Valentine demands.

James clears his throat and prepares to present his manifesto. He stands up straight and cracks his knuckles. Dark bags persist under both of James's eyes and red spots are scattered throughout the rest of his face. He looks like he hasn't slept in months.

"Gentlemen, I have crafted a new law that will make New Haven even better than good!"

"Uh oh," says Valentine.

"It's called Pillars of a New Way!" he says as he pushes piles of papers in each of their directions. "Here you go. Read it and be amazed!"

Lester picks up one of the loose papers and starts to read it silently. Valentine does the same.

Not a minute goes by before Lester and Valentine both glance at each other for a moment and then burst out into laughter.

"What is so funny?" James demands.

They continue laughing only harder now. Lester wipes a tear from his cheek.

"Why are you laughing? Why are- I have created a masterpiece here. And... and you won't even look at it."

"James, you can't be serious here," says Lester as he picks up another stray piece of paper and reads it out loud.

"All women are to be placed on leashes as they walk about the neighborhoods."

"Would they be like dogs?" he asks. Did you want them to lick their assess and bark too?"

"Wait, wait, wait!" says Valentine, laughing out loud. "This one here says A woman cannot eat without seeking her husband's approval first. I actually kinda like that one."

"James. Come on. Please. Alright, you lost your girl, and now you're upset. It's mildly understandable. But we can't implement this crap!

James frowns and hangs his head.

"I mean, come on! Leashes? Curfews? We'll start losing even more international support if we go this radical," Lester says as he turns to Valentine.

"I'm done with you wasting my time," says Valentine. "Thanks for the laugh but this meeting is over."

"Wait! But… just… hold on. I- I think this could really change things!" he pleads as they continue walking toward the door. "Don't you see guys? We're losing our grip on the women. They're breaking the rules! We have to…"

Valentine and Lester leave the room, and James's words bounce off the closed door. He feels defeated. He appeared to have hit rock bottom when Sybil left, but this feels like a whole new level. Embarrassment. Now he truly has nothing. He feels worthless. Undiscovered. Like a diamond in the rough. At least it's Friday.

James drags his feet back to his floor where Cyrus is waiting for him. The Workplace is almost entirely cleared out as everyone is going home for the day.

"Hey! How'd it go in there boss?"

James picks up his head. He lacks the energy and excitement from before and loosely holds the papers of his manifesto as they dangle from his fingertips. "Great. Just great," he says walking past Cyrus and toward his office. Some of the papers he's holding fall to the floor.

Cyrus bends down to help pick them up. "Cool. So…"

"I don't get why no one takes me seriously here," says James cutting Cyrus off. "I try and I try again, and nothing ever seems…"

"Hey uh- James… Sir," he interrupts. "Why don't we talk about this on our way to The Palace?"

James perks up. "You're going?"

"Of course, I'm going. It's fucking Friday," says Cyrus enthusiastically as he pats James on the back. "Come on, well hop in your shuttle and hang out. Decompress. Something tells me you could use a good night out. What do you say boss?"

James looks at Cyrus for a moment. He can't tell if he is just a nice guy or if he wants something out of him. But he dreads going home again to an empty house.

"Alright. Fine. Let's do it," James says, cracking a soft smile. "Meet you outside in ten."

***

James and Cyrus enter the shuttle and take off from the parking pad just outside The Workplace. They travel through the air in silence for the first few minutes, both looking out the windows of the shuttle at the grey everlasting landscape of New Haven. Life still goes on below.

"Wish we had some music in here," Cyrus says. After the sentence leaves his lips, he tightens his face, and tenses his jaw. "Oh shit."

"Relax. It's ok," James says. "I loved music once. They don't monitor the shuttles."

Cyrus blows air from his mouth. "Phew. I hope not."

"Sometimes I miss the way things were," James says. "You're probably too young to remember."

"Well, I've heard things," says Cyrus. "But this isn't so bad. I mean The Palace is pretty sweet."

James doesn't reply and continues looking out the window. He taps on the glass with his finger and then sits up straight facing Cyrus.

"I wish I could just fucking leave."

Cyrus's mouth opens wide. His eyes dart around the small cabin of the shuttle. "Uh. What do you mean?"

"I. Wish. I. Could. Fucking. Leave," he repeats in pieces as he looks back out the window.

Cyrus bites his lip. "What? Are you serious? You actually… want to leave?"

"Yeah. I think so."

"Where would you go?"

James looks back at Cyrus and lightly shakes his head. "Never mind. Just forget I said anything. I'm just venting."

Cyrus continues staring at James. It looks like he wants to speak but no words are coming out.

James shifts uncomfortably in his seat. "If you tell anyone I said that, ill fucking kill you."

Cyrus doesn't reply. His eyes are wide and shifting side to side. He's thinking.

"Hello? Cyrus? Can you hear me? What the fuck?"

"Where would you go?" Cyrus says again. "Tell me."

"What? Why?"

"Because what if…" he sighs. "What if I could get you there?"

James wrinkles his brow.

"Cyrus what the fuck are you saying? Don't fuck with me."

The shuttle begins to descend from the air as they approach the landing pad of The Palace.

"Where would you go?" Cyrus says again. "Hurry."

"North. I would go north," James says shifting around. "Are you saying you can get me there?"

"Yeah. I can. I know a guy that can help us. But it's not a guarantee."

James frowns and drops his shoulders.

"Yet."

The shuttle lands on the pad and the door opens as the cabin depressurizes. Cyrus and James look at each other and speak only with their eyes as they stand up and exit.

"Later." James whispers.

Cyrus nods.

"For now, let's go have some fun."

13 RUN

12 hours earlier

Sybil sprints toward a small water plane, hand in hand with Cameron. As she approaches the plane, which sits on the Lake Simmons shore, she can't help but notice the innumerable dings and scratches that decorate the entire body of the aircraft.

Will this thing even fly?

She inhales the night air. It's thick and smells rich of gasoline. The moon looks down on her, offering small orbs of light as it peaks through the slowly drifting clouds. Patches of sand and granules of rock support the planes pair of wheels as they sit idlily, engulfed with loads of potential energy.

"We've got to get in the clouds!" the pilot yells over the screaming of the engine. "Hurry now!"

Cam grabs the handle of the door and swings it open against the force of the wind. He takes one step into the cabin and reaches his hand back for Sybil's. He helps her inside and the door slams thunderously behind them.

"Buckle up!" yells the pilot as he places a headset on his ears and faces the dashboard.

The engine roars as the plane moves from land to water. It picks up speed and starts to skirt along the surface. Bouncing as it goes. Sybil holds on tight to Cam's bicep as the plane elevates. They ascend into the inky sky. They are almost free.

Cameron made arrangements with the pilot over a month ago, as he waited patiently for Sybil to choose him over James. On a late-night session at The Nerve, Sybil confided her feelings about leaving James. She ranted on how James was acting differently recently. That he had become intoxicated with power and influence and that she couldn't recognize him any longer. She told Cam that she was ready to run away with him, and here they are. Floating on a plane in the middle of the night. Escaping their personal tortures.

The plane continues to jounce as it pierces through the clouds. Silence dominates the cabin of the plane, as it abounds with nervous energy.

"We've got around 150 miles before we hit the border," says the pilot. "I'll let you know when it's safe."

"If we were going to get shot down, it would have happened already, right?" asks Cam.

"No," replies the pilot. "It would happen right about now."

The plane jostles and bends sharp to the right. The forces from the sudden adjustment contort Sybil's stomach into enough knots to tie a thousand shoes. She yelps and buries her face into Cam's shoulder.

They continue to climb and increase speed. The turbulence intensifies as the cabin shakes violently. Whooshing sounds and high pitches screeches dominate the ambiance.

"Hey!" yells Sybil. "Is this normal?"

"Just hang on."

Sybil holds onto Cam as they count the seconds. Tighter and tighter becomes her grasp. She feels her chest rise and fall with the rapid pace of her breath and her head becomes hot and tense. She closes her eyes as the plane wobbles back and forth. It dips and dives, as it picks up great speed. Sybil wishes she were home, in her bed with James. Even if it were back in New Haven. The sounds of the engine get louder and more strained. The noise is booming and building to a grand crescendo. But then, the plane beings to steady. The clamoring noises that had just invoked intense fear are drifting. And then gone.

Silence.

"So… the weather… am I right?" Cam says, projecting his voice.

Sybil exhales into a laugh and playfully slaps his arm.

"Sorry about that, folks. Can't control the skies."

Cam and Sybil look at each other and relax their grips.

"I hope you guys are hungry," says the pilot, changing the subject. "Much better cuisine up north."

"Well, I was hungry earlier but I'm afraid your flying has destroyed my appetite," says Sybil.

"More for me!" Cam says. "Ugh. I'm dying for a steak."

"Well, you're in luck. There's a smoked meat place downtown called Steiner's that's unbelievable. It's a sandwich on rye with horseradish, mustard, pickles, and all that, but the meat is so tender it melts away in your mouth."

Sybil smiles at Cam. "Ok, I'm hungry again."

"Hey, Thomas, who is waiting for us on the other side?" Asks Cam.

"There's a refugee camp over there- actually there's tons of them now. They call themselves The Skyline. They're all a bunch of ex-pats from New Haven that made it out alive. They organize themselves into groups and then they hire guys like me to sneak out here to grab good folks like you."

"Well, we're certainly grateful," says Cam. "Why do you do it?"

Thomas smiles and rubs his fingers together.

"Don't thank me till we touch down at the border," says Thomas. "About 100 miles to go."

The plane continues through the late-night sky, so far undetected by New Haven airspace control. This particular route was carefully picked and planned by the Skyline team. They base their routes off of Leadership air traffic habits and shift changes. This compiles into a 32% successful extraction percentage which Cam chose to leave out from his conversation with Sybil. All she knew is that they would run away north to be together, and that James would be left behind.

The wheels touch dirt at four thirty-five in the morning at the border between New Haven and New America. Sybil, Cam, and Thomas are greeted at the door by three women and one man; all wearing the same uniforms with large aviation symbols plastered on their shirts. They're led into a large, unmarked van where they meet other refugees from Brightwater and other surrounding factions.

"It's nice to meet all of you. My name is Hunter, and I'd like to welcome

131

you to New America. This is Rachel, Gen, and Hannah and we are part of a collective that is working to free New Haven. We are Skyline. You will all be set up with a temporary residence and job interviews, as well as some provisions that should last you a few weeks. It's a 2 and a half-hour drive to the holding facility so sit tight. We will brief you all from there."

Sybil looks around at all the other refugees curious to see if any familiar faces would appear. They all look tired and worn and three times their ages. She notices a baby sitting quietly on a woman's lap in the back of the van. The baby is bundled up from head to toe and sleeping in her mother's arms. Sybil glances over and makes eye contact with the mother.

"One day," Cam says as he grabs Sybil's hand.

***

The van arrives at an enormous office building that has been fully renovated into a holding facility for refugees. It's as wide as it is tall and is painted bright blue on the outside. The front of the building says HOLDING in big, black, and bold lettering. The van pulls into one of many spots at the head of the building along with a few other vehicles that are also carrying refugees. Everyone unloads and coalesces on the sidewalk in front of the building. As Sybil takes her first steps onto the pavement, she's hit with a wave of the thin, and wispy northern air. She notices that it isn't all that much different than New Haven; although the smell of smoke and bustling factories is gone and is replaced by something much more subtle and fresh.

Wintergreen?

"Alright everyone. In a moment, we will go into the holding facility for processing. It's not scary or anything, well just take your fingerprints and such," says Hunter. Please grab your bags and follow me."

The refugees follow Hunter into the lobby of the holding facility. The revolving front doors reveal architecture that resembles an older but classically designed hotel. The lobby is a large square space with white leather couches and console tables stationed off to either side. A giant fountain of an angel boasts from the center of the room as water falls all around it. The flooring is luxury vinyl tile, that is accented with multicolored stains of paint. Sybil notices many colorful art pieces hanging from the walls as their colors blend brilliantly with the reflections of light that bounce off the floor.

"This place seems magical," Sybil whispers to Cam as she grips the inside of his arm.

Cam nods and looks curiously around the lobby as the refugees file in.

Hunter is at the front of the pack and stops at the fountain while everyone makes their way inside. "Everyone, please form two lines separated by gender. Men to the left. Woman and children to the right."

Cam hands Sybil her bag as they part to join the two lines that are quickly forming. Another man in a Skyline uniform joins Hunter by the fountain and waits for everyone to get settled. The sounds of rushing footsteps and falling water fill the air. Hunter moves to stand in front of Sybil's line as the other man stands in front of the men. They're positioned at small podiums and hold clipboards as they count the heads of everyone standing in front of them. Sybil glances over at Cam in the other line and can't help but laugh as he's sandwiched between the stomachs of two large men.

The line continues moving and Sybil eventually arrives at the podium. She places her index finger down on the scanner. It pauses, beeps twice and turns green.

"Alright, smile for the camera," Hunter says as he holds a tablet in front of her face.

Sybil cracks a small and awkward smile.

Click.

"Now, sign here," he instructs, sliding the tablet forward.

Sybil sees her picture next to a field of words. She frowns at the sight of her face and scribbles down her name quickly.

"Next!" he shouts as he motions for her to move forward.

She walks forward and stops at a door in the back of the lobby where another man in Skyline uniform is waiting for her. She sees Cam and the rest of the men stopping at a different door across the lobby.

"Right this way ma'am," he says. He opens the door to a field of small offices in a solidly white and elongated room. This room is devoid of color. Each office is marked with a black number on the top of its door from one to eight.

"Go to station number four please," the man directs. Sybils nods and heads to the fourth office. She stops at the plain white door.

"Come in," says a voice from the inside.

Sybil turns the handle and opens the door to see a small and thin brunette with glasses, sitting at a desk. She holds a tablet in her hands and is reading from it silently.

"Hello Mrs...."

"Harker," she says. "Sybil Harker."

"Right. Mrs. Harker. Welcome to our facility. I'm Veronica with Skyline and we're happy that you're here. We're going to have a conversation now if that's alright. I need to get to know you just a bit before I can let you go on your way. Sounds good?"

"Yes. That's fine."

"Brilliant. So, what made you take the leap of faith?"

"Pardon me?" Sybil asks. "What... leap of faith."

"Well coming here of course! It's a tough task getting out from where you've come. As you know, it's often unsuccessful. What made you take such a risk not knowing if you would come out of it alive?"

Sybil thinks for a moment before responding.

"Well, for starters I hated it there. They tried to kill me and marked me as a traitor."

"I see," says Veronica pushing her glasses into her face. "Are you a traitor?"

"No. No I am not."

"Right. So, what are your goals for your new life here? Anything you hope to accomplish."

"Well, I've come here with someone. My frien- husband," Sybil says. "He was in the other line. With the men."

"Yes, yes. A Mr. Cameron Harker?"

"Yes."

"And the two of you are married?"

"Yes."

"Officially?"

"Yes. Well, not yet. But we will be," says Sybil biting her lip.

"I see," says Veronica as she uses her finger to scroll on the tablet. "And why not yet?"

Sybil brushes her hair back from her face. "I had a husband. Before. In New Haven," she says. "But I've left him behind. For good."

Veronica tightens her gaze. "And if he comes looking for you? What if he were to track you back here?"

"He won't. He can't," she says emphatically.

Veronica squints her eyes as she looks hard at Sybil.

"He's dead."

Veronica sits back in her chair and folds her arms. "Oh, I'm so sorry. That must make you quite sad."

"Yes. Sometimes. But I am happy to be here with Cam though. You all are so nice for bringing us in. I promise you; we won't cause any trouble," she says, looking at Veronica intently but offering a soft closed lip smile.

"I don't believe you will," says Veronica glancing back down at the tablet. She clicks a few buttons on the screen and puts it down on the table.

"You're free to go," she says. "You can wait for Cameron in your room. Someone just outside will guide you."

"Thank you," Sybil replies.

Veronica stands and outstretches her hand. Sybil flinches at first but then reaches out and shakes it firmly.

***

After the processing, Cam and Sybil meet in their room on the 8th floor of the building. It comes fully equipped with food, cable television, and medical supplies. Sybil is used to having things taken care of for her in New Haven, however something feels different here. It feels as if she has more of a choice in what she will be doing. They have set up job interviews for her at various facilities, but she has the choice after all in which one she will take. There is no mandatory assignment to The Fund. There is no PC card. She will be earning real paper money that she can keep in a bank or under her mattress if she wants. This is exciting for Sybil, but at the same time, she can feel a sense of anxiety brewing from the depths of her gut.

"Well, this will do," Cam says as he falls backwards onto the king-sized bed.

"I can't believe we really did this," says Sybil. "I'm so happy."

Cam leans over to Sybil and kisses her. Once. And then again. And then again, before they settle in the comfort of each other's arms.

"There's no one in this whole world, that I've ever loved, like I love you," she whispers. "I don't care what happens over the next few weeks. As long we're together."

"Yeah exactly," he responds. "We'll figure everything out. We'll get jobs, we'll start our lives. We'll have a million children. I'll be a barista!" he says laughing. "Don't you think I'd make a good cup of coffee?"

"The best," Sybil says.

They fall asleep in each other's arms and don't wake until the very next morning when a knock at the door interrupts their honeymoon. It's Hunter.

"I brought some clothing for your interviews today; in case you didn't bring any from home," says Hunter. "Sybil, you will be interviewing to be a paralegal at the Bernfield law firm. Cam, your interview is with Ace's marketing."

"All right! Marketing. Sounds good to me," says Cam enthusiastically as he looks eagerly at Sybil. "If I can sell sex, I can sell... whatever they have over there."

"A ride will pick you both up in the front of the facility in an hour. So, get dressed!"

The two of them throw on the clothes that Hunter has provided them and make their way downstairs to their transport. They kiss goodbye and file into their respective vehicles.

Sybil arrives at the Bernfield law firm and sits down in the waiting room. It's an extremely busy waiting room with men and women all dressed professionally.

I guess there's some competition.

"Sybil Hawkin... erm, Harkin," says the receptionist.
Sybil stands.

"Mr. Bernfield will see you now."

She follows the receptionist down an exceptionally long hallway and up to an office in the corner of the building.

"Good luck," she says as she knocks on the door and scampers off.

"Yes," says a grumbly voice from the inside.

Sybil turns the handle of the door and enters the office to find a short, stubby, and balding man sitting at a computer screen.

"Hello, sir. It's nice to meet you. I'm Sybil Clear- Harkin! Uh. I'm here for the job int-"

"Yes, yes. Mrs. Kilharkin. Nice to meet you. Sit down already."

Sybil hurries to sit in the seat in front of Mr. Bernfield's desk. "It appears he is in a sour mood. He fidgets in his seat and picks up an unlit cigar from his desk. He lights it and inhales, sending smoke all over the room.

"We're hiring 30 people for 2 positions for god's sake," he blurts out. "Listen, I'm all for you refugees finding freedom and whatnot, and I'm not a racist or anything. But at some point, we gotta start looking out for our own. Know what I mean?"

Sybil quickly moves her eyes around the office. "Uh, sir, I-"

"Or else, there won't be any jobs left for the locals! We'll end up being staffed entirely by foreigners by the end of the year, and then what? What are we supposed to do?"

He takes another puff of the cigar.

"Well, erm, maybe there could be-"

"It's all so damn political these days," he cuts in.

Sybil drops her head.

This fucking guy.

"Listen here, New America will be the next New Haven, just you see. All this bullshit. Sometimes it's hard to take it laying down. Know what I mean?"

He kicks his feet up on the desk and leans back with his hands behind his head.

"Yes," Sybil responds.

"Plus, war's gonna be starting soon anyway. Which side do you wanna be on?"

"Yours, sir."

"That's damn right! Hey, I like you, Sybil. You're not half bad. Not like them other folks, all PC and shit. Sometimes I wonder who has a brain in their heads these days. You want the job? I'm sick of interviews anyways. Know what I mean?"

"Yes."

"Great! Welcome aboard. Any questions?"

"What do you mean war is going to be starting soon?" Sybil asks.

"Oh, nobody told you? That sick country of yours is fucked! We've been preparing for war with New Haven for years now, and I think now, it's finally happening. Maybe in the next few weeks. They talk about it on the news all the time. Oh, shit, sorry. Do you know what the news is?"

"Yes, I know what the news is. I just haven't seen it in a while."

"We'll you're not missing much anyways," he says crossing his arms. "Other than China being China and that shithole that used to be America causing international trouble. Know what I mean?"

"What kinds of interna-"

"Great so welcome aboard like I said. And uh- give Julissa your information on your way out. I'm very busy."

"Al-alright," she says standing up. "Thank you, sir."

An hour goes by, and Sybil returns to the hotel room where Cam is there waiting for her.

"Hey. How did it go love?" he asks as she walks through the door.

"Well, I guess I got the job," she says as she puts her bag down on the floor.

"Wow! We're here five minutes and you're already employed."

"Yeah, he's kind of mean though. I don't know, we'll see," she says, sitting down on the bed. "How does it go with you?"

"Ah, I'll try my luck tomorrow."

"Why what happened?"

"I don't know, they didn't seem interested in me," he says, folding his hands. "I tried to ask them how to follow up, but they gave me the whole, thanks for coming in, we'll call you, routine. Whatever."

"Aw, that's alright. You'll find something soon."

"Well, we better because I've got nothing left from New Haven. They've likely drained my account and given it to James, now that they know we defected."

"It's alright, we don't need any of that. I'll be the breadwinner in this relationship, and you can be the stay-at-home-mom," she teases.

"All I need is you," he says, rubbing her back.

"Listen, I'm gonna go take a shower and freshen up, why don't you start thinking about dinner. Maybe Hunter can give us some recommendations," she says.

"Good plan. I'll go find him," he says as he starts for the door.

Sybil closes the door to the bathroom and rests both of her hands on the counter. She slowly raises her head to make eye contact with herself in the mirror. Unexpectedly, she starts to cry and places her hand over her mouth so that no one can hear her weep. She wipes the tears from her eyes and stands up straight.

This better work.

She moves away from the mirror and turns the shower on until it is scalding hot. The steam fills up the room and she fades into the mist.

14 A LEAP OF FAITH

James arrives to work late the next morning. His face is sullen. He looks mainly at the floor. Observing his gait. Preparing for another day of routine. The slide takes him to his floor, and he walks toward his office with heavy steps. He reaches for the handle of his office door when he notices a small white envelope lodged halfway underneath it. James wrinkles his brow and looks behind him. He glances around the office space, but nobody is looking back. He bends over and grabs the envelope. It's plain and white with no writing on it. Not even his name. He opens the door and sits down at his desk. He holds the envelope in his hands directly in front of him and considers just throwing it away.

I can't handle any other problems right now.

He holds it up to the light and tries to make out what's inside. The light reveals a folded piece of paper inside with what looks like dark black writing. His curiosity overcomes him as and rips the envelope open, revealing a handwritten note on yellow binder paper. It reads:

James, $250,000 has been wired from Cameron Harker's PC and transferred to yours. These funds are now available.

- Leadership

His eyes dart around the room as he thinks for a moment before he crumples up the note and disposes it in the shredder. His expression morphs into an uncontrollable smile before he quickly closes his mouth. His heart starts to race, and his palms stick. His eyes close and a large breath escapes his lips that his nerves chop into small pieces.

Its go time.

James steps out of his office and runs to find Cyrus who is at his desk talking with Harry.

"Cyrus! Hey," he says catching his breath.

"Hey boss, what's going-"

"The child traffickers! Uh, the traffic- what-what's the status of that investigation? With the child traffickers?"

Cyrus's eyes widen at the question.

"Child traffickers?" Harry asks.

"Oh. I'm glad you asked sir," says Cyrus standing up. Let me gather my things and I'll meet you in the War-Room."

Harry wrinkles his brow and sits back in his chair confused.

"No need," says James. "Just brief the Squad like we talked about and put the address and meeting time on my desk. I need to go prep. Oh, and keep Arayah back here. For… recon."

"On it," says Cyrus, as James hurries back to his office.

"Who is trafficking children?" asks Harry.

"Oh, ho-ho. Just you wait. it's a huge operation mate. Could be a big score for all of us," says Cyrus. "Let's go find Cruz."

***

Fifteen hours later, James meets Cyrus, Harry, and the newest member of squad B, Cruz, at vehicle storage.

"Alright boys the time has come. It's going to be a good night," James says as he zips up his jacket and approaches the crew.

"Cyrus you and I will take a stinger, and you two will operate the tank," James commands. "The address is already loaded into everyone's GPS. You will follow what it says and do exactly as you're told. We cannot afford to get lost."

"Why do we need a tank?" asks Cruz. "Are we going to be fight-"

"Yes, sir," says Cyrus looking hard at Cruz. "That's how you reply. You do as you're told, and you don't ask questions."

Cruz straightens up. "Yes sir."

Cyrus flashes a smile. "Great. Now listen up. James and I will come from the east, and you guys will come from the west. We'll clamp down on them, and they'll have nowhere to run. Cool? Remember, children are at stake here," says Cyrus. "We can't mess this up."

Cruz opens his mouth to speak when Harry steps in front of him cutting him off. "Sounds good."

The four men break and go to their respective vehicles. James gets in the driver's seat as Cyrus sits beside him.

"You ready to do this?" says James looking straight ahead.

"God, I hope this works."

"Me too."

The engine of the stinger rumbles as they exit the lot turning left. The tank behind them holding Harry and Cruz turns right.

10 minutes of silence go by as the cabin of the stinger collects an abundant aura of nerves. James looks down at the clock. It reads 11:26 PM.

"We're making good time. Any chance we're too early?" asks James.

"No, we're doing good," says Cyrus. "Drive slower."

The men continue in the darkness of the night with only headlights and a GPS to guide them.

The tank carrying Harry and Cruz approaches the preloaded address. They barrel into a quiet residential neighborhood for plebs. The reinforced tracks of the tank roll effortlessly over gravel. Small apartment-like buildings that are stacked on top of each other peak out hauntingly from the darkness and fog. There is such little space between the apartments that only a single person could fit inside the width of the alley. There are no parking spots or mailboxes or even anything that you would find in a traditional New Haven slum. This project was built for the poorest of the poor. The most desperate of the desperados. The tank slows to a stop as they wait for instruction.

James and Cyrus slowly pull up to the top of a small hill overlooking a harbor. There are multiple docks out ahead. Most of them empty and some with small pontoon boats and catamarans left unoccupied.

"Alright, let's go," says James.

They exit the stinger carefully with weapons drawn. The hill is dark aside from the shades of moonlight that bounce off the water. James and Cyrus look around carefully at their immediate surroundings for signs of a threat.

"I think we're clear," says Cyrus.

"Good."

James grabs a large black duffel bag out of the trunk and proceeds to walk down the hill. As James becomes distant, Cyrus carefully places four bricks of C12 explosives on each seat of the stinger before closing the doors and running to catch up with James.

As the two men move side by side down the hill and closer to the dock, Cyrus notices a small group of people on the midnight shoreline.

"Wait!" he says, placing his hand on James's chest to slow him down. "Check that out." Cyrus points to the group of people.

"Bingo," says James. "Follow my lead."

***

Harry and Cruz grow impatient as they stand in silence around the tank.

"Let's just call them bro," says Cruz. "How long we gonna wait for?"

Harry nods and speaks into his earpiece.

"I think we've made it to the neighborhood. Are you guys close on the other side?"

"Yeah, we're close," replies James. "Go ahead and advance, we're coming around the backside."

Harry and Cruz draw their guns and approach the apartment building. They gingerly advance up the rusty metal stairs as each step clanks in the silence of the night. The sky is pitch black and decorated with only fractions of light from a moon that is very far away.

"I still don't get why we needed a tank," whispers Cruz.

"Shh! We're close," says Harry climbing the stairs. "Room 512, right?"

"Uh- yeah 512," says Cruz.

They ascend to the 5th floor and stop at the top of the stairs.

"Okay, let's wait here for a moment for them to catch up," says Harry as the two of them tuck away behind a guardrail.

Cyrus and James close in on the small group of people standing by the shoreline.

"I count seven. Mostly men I think," says James. "Where do you think they-"

He's interrupted by a huge force smashing him and Cyrus to the ground. Black bags are forced over their heads as their hands are forced behind their backs.

"Names!" demands a voice.

"AHH! WHAT THE FUCK! HELP!" James screams. His words muffle awkwardly through the bag that is intimate with his face.

"It's me!" yells Cyrus. "It's me! Veritas! Veritas!"

"Ah-ha! I win," says a voice as the bags lift from their faces.

"Shit," says the other one.

"You win what? Asks Cyrus, fixing his hair.

"I bet Curly here that it was you and that cop you said you were bringing up on the hill. He said you'd never be that stupid! Ha! Walkin' around all spy like with your guns."

"You called me a cop?" James asks Cyrus.

"Oh, he called you much worse," says one of the men laughing.

"That's not- were not- whatever," says Cyrus. "Were here. You guys tackled us, ha-ha. Can we get going now?" he says taking the earpiece out of his ear.

"Don't worry officer Jamie. I didn't believe all that shit he was saying about you," says one of the men smiling and putting his arm around James.

"Any friend of Cyrus is a friend of mine. Welcome, brother. We better get on the boat. It's time to go."

***

"Guys, are you in position? It's time to move!" whispers Harry into the earpiece.

Silence.

"Guys, what's going on? Do you hear me?"

Still no reply.

"James, Cyrus, are you there?" Cruz asks getting close to Harry's ear so he could be heard.

"Fuck why are they not answering?" asks Harry.

"Well, what the hell do we do, man? What if they got caught or something? I don't wanna die, man, this is my first mission. Let's go back, man!" Cruz pleads.

"No, fuck that. We're here to do a job, we do the job. Follow me to the doorway."

Cruz throws his head back and rolls his eyes as he follows Harry to the door of 512. They both rest on either side of the handle.

"Okay, look. I'm going to open the door with this pick, and then you get ready to throw the stunner as soon as you have enough room. You good?" says Harry.

"Fine fucker. Let's do this," says Cruz.

Harry picks the lock and swings the door open. Cruz grabs a grenade from his tactical belt and tosses it inside the room.

BANG

Smoke engulfs the room as Harry and Cruz struggle to see.

"You threw a smoke grenade, you idiot!" yells Harry between fits of coughing.

"Hands up!" squeaks Cruz, his lungs hacking. "Hands up if you can hear me!"

They advance their way forward ducking through the thick smokey air.

As the smoke begins to clear, Harry and Cruz see a horrified Hispanic-looking mother tightly gripping her two small children as they huddle together on a small cot in the corner of the room.

"Who the fuck are they?" says Harry.

"Vato, I got this." Cruz clears his throat.

"Who are you?" He asks, slowly emphasizing each word.

The mother shakes her head in confusion as pulls her children tighter.

"Como te.. uh shit.. como se llama...tos?" says Cruz in broken Spanish.

Harry smacks Cruz on the back of the head.

"Lo siento, lo siento," Harry says as he backs out of the room, grabbing Cruz by the arm to lead him out.

"What bro? She probably only knows Spanish. What are you doing?"

"They fucked us VATO!" Harry yells mocking Cruz as he closes the door to 512.

"Huh? What you mean? We didn't even interrogate her yet."

"Not her you dumb fucking asshole! James and Cyrus. They-"

"Wait" interrupts Cruz. You're saying they gave us the wrong address on purpose? Why so they can get credit for the raid themselves?"

"I don't know Cruz. I'm here experiencing this WITH you. I don't know why they- oh shit. Yeah, they were acting weird about this child trafficking thing."

Cruz smiles. "Let's go get those bitches then vatito!"

***

James and Cyrus board a small boat along with the men that they met at the shoreline. As the boat leaves the harbor, James looks down at his watch and presses a button that places the Stinger that's currently sitting at the top of the hill in neutral. It crosses over the edge of the hill and starts to roll down, picking up speed until it violently crashes into the water below.

"Now," says James.

Cyrus produces a small device from his pocket and activates it. At that moment, the Stinger explodes into a million pieces sending shrapnel flying everywhere. The fiery flames rise from the vehicle and illuminate the water. They're just out of reach from the explosion as they look on with satisfaction.

The boat advances to open water where they meet a waterplane piloted by a member of The Railroad. James and Cyrus board the plane and take their seats among the rest of the men. James clutches his black duffel tightly to his chest as the propellers of the plane begin to spin.

"Everyone ready to go?" the pilot asks.

"Let's go Thomas," says Cyrus as the plane lifts off the water and soars into the sky.

15 THE BEGINNING OF THE END

.

James bows his head as he exits the plane to a relieving ray of sunshine that strikes his eyes. He clutches the black duffel tight to his chest as he descends a narrow set of stairs. The darkness that had occupied the night has since shifted and the early morning sun has just begun to show its face. James touches new ground.

"This way sir," says one of the rescuers waving her hand as she leads all the passengers to a waiting station.

James files in line and notices a couple of other planes that have recently landed on the runway. He sees passengers just like himself, rushing out to freedom. It appears this is a larger operation than he had originally thought.

I'm a refugee.

James is brought to a centralized meeting zone right outside of the airport. Hundreds of people scatter as they find their loved ones and embrace at first sight. Husbands are reunited with their wives. Children with their parents. And friends with friends after absences of far too long.

"You sure you made contact," James says to Cyrus, nervously looking on through the mess of people.

"Yeah, I'm sure," replies Cyrus trudging along, trying to keep up with James's pace.

James inches closer to the meeting zone as countless amounts of people intercept his sights. It's at that moment, through a mess of individuals, that James finally sees her, looking back at him through the maze. James tosses his bag into Cyrus's chest and pushes through a mess of people. Sybil does the same before leaps into his arms.

Cyrus, watches from behind them and breathes a long sigh of relief.

"I knew it. I just knew it!" Sybil says through her tears.

"I know love, I know. We made it," he says, holding her tight.

Sybil loosens her grip. "Did you get the money?"

James laughs and motions for Cyrus. He retrieves the black duffel and unzips the bag revealing piles and piles of NHBs.

"There's enough here for all of us," James says to the group as he pinches Cyrus's shoulder. He closes the bag and hangs it over his shoulder. "We wouldn't be here without this guy."

Sybil flashes a smile and hugs Cyrus briefly.

"Come on, I'll take you two love birds to the safehouse."

Cyrus directs them to a parking lot near the meeting zone. Its filled with old cars from years back that have collected dust and dirt from seemingly years of sitting idle. They approach an old blue car near the front with rusted mirrors and faded paint. Cyrus reaches under the left back tire and retrieves a set of keys.

"Bingo," he says as he opens the car doors for James and Sybil who sit together in the backseat.

"This should do," James says with a scrunched-up face like he smells rotten eggs.

Cyrus laughs and gets into the driver's seat.

"It's only about a 30-minute drive from here so don't get too comfy."

***

The old blue car pulls off the street and onto a side road hidden between the trees. The car jumps and bumps with every rock. Nothing but overgrown foliage surrounds them as they slow to an even pace.

"Almost there," says Cyrus. "Hang on."

James and Sybil exchange looks.

After a few minutes of uncomfortable silence and nausea, a clearing in the trees comes into view as the brush shrinks thinner.

The car suddenly hangs a right turn and at that moment, brand new scenery appears. The closed in spaces of the brush and rocky road are quickly replaced with wide open plains of land and what appears to be a functioning farm.

"Oh wow," Sybil says.

Cyrus smiles as he pulls the car in front of the property. "Welcome home guys."

The car comes to a halt and James rolls down the window. The air is thin, and sweet with hints of manure that quickly turn his senses sour. He sees goats, chickens, and cows roaming free around the property and bites his cheek. There is a group of people standing by a two-story house next to a barn that start to approach the car. James rolls up the window.

"Let's just hang tight for a second and let Jeremy come check us out," says Cyrus.

As they wait in the car, James notices that the safehouse's property is littered with revolutionaries organized into what appears to be a militia. They stand outside, laced in camo, and armed beyond any military fanatic's wildest dreams.

Jeremy is holding an assault rifle by his side as he approaches the car in even, military-like strides. He arrives at the car and bends over his tall frame to look inside the driver's window. He sees Cyrus and nods his head without changing his expression. He systematically patrols around the car and then inspects the backseat window where he sees James and Sybil. He steps back from the car and motions to Cyrus to come forward.

"Clear!" he yells.

"Alright guys, let's go," says Cyrus.

The doors open and James and Sybil position themselves by the car while Cyrus goes to talk with Jeremy.

James notices Jeremy's frame is massive. He is muscular with short red hair and clearly has some sort of army experience. He wears black boots, jeans and a white T-shirt that furiously grips his skin.

"What's the status on Cam?" asks James bluntly.

Sybil appears shocked for a moment. "Erm. He - he's dealt with," She snaps.

"Good," he says, straightening his back and stiffening his posture.

Jeremy shakes hands with Cyrus and returns to the car with a woman.

"My friends. Welcome to the safehouse. I am Jeremy, your host and this is Bonnie your guide. She will take you to your rooms and answer any questions that you might have."

"Sir, I can take your bag," Bonnie says to James.

"Bag stays with me," he replies sharply. James makes eye contact with Jeremy. "But- but thank you."

Bonnie leads James and Sybil inside the main house while Cyrus stays outside to talk with his old friend. The house is quaint but old and looks like it hadn't been updated in years. An old scruffy leather couch is centered in the middle of the living room with a dirty coffee table wearing cigarette buts all over it.

"Sorry for the... appearance," says Bonnie. "We do with what we have. Your room is just right this way."

As the cross the living room, James notices the TV is on and stops to listen.

"The tensions continue to grow globally and there's not much time for evacuation," says a reporter on the screen.

"Wait, wait, wait, what is he saying?" says Sybil. "Turn it up."

Bonnie grabs the remote from the couch and turns the volume louder.

"I have just gotten word, and I am afraid to say, we are officially at war with New Haven."

ABOUT THE AUTHOR

Dr. Adam Kirstein is a dedicated medical doctor with a deep love for both his family and the challenges life presents. He shares his home with his wife, Alena Kirstein, and their cats, Boots and Sansa.

Beyond his medical practice, Dr. Kirstein finds joy in writing, inventing, and playing chess. He's an avid sports enthusiast and enjoys embracing life's myriad opportunities.

Dr. Kirstein invites you to discover his debut novel, where he shares his unique perspective and a touch of his passion for storytelling.

PERSONAL THOUGHTS

I thought of the idea for this book whilst in the shower of all places. That's where I find myself most in thought. I think that the precipitating factor for these ideas was a distaste, that I felt at that time and most certainly feel today, for the government and their blatant tactics of manipulation and lies.

As George Orwell saw all those years ago, I believe that we haven't strayed very far from the path of slowly becoming cogs in a great big wheel. One that churns away at the hopes and dreams of the unfortunate. One that circulates money and sells happiness. One that cares not for the people but for production, as they have trained a land of zombie consumerism and ousted anyone or anything in their way. Without repercussion. Without foul. The hypocrisy is abundant. You need only look.

I've come to believe that this world is all one big game. That the rules that we, as a society have come to live by, have all been made by men and enforced by men, thus they can be changed by men; so long as there is courage and conviction.

This is not so much a negative thought as that may be your initial persuasion. For me, it has been quite freeing actually. I now feel that there is nothing beyond the realm of immediate possibility. That you can write books, make things that other people use, run for office, ask for forgiveness, ace a test, fail a test, eat a donut, run a race, BE YOURSELF. You are free to make choices in this life so why not make some fun ones.

We are only here but for a second.

New Haven

Hi <3

Printed in Great Britain
by Amazon

33928896R00098